Let Heaven Fall

LET HEAVEN FALL

Amy Pirnie

Constable • London

Constable & Robinson Ltd
3 The Lanchesters
162 Fulham Palace Road
London W6 9ER
www.constablerobinson.com

First published in the UK by Allison & Busby 1994

This edition published in the UK by Constable,
an imprint of Constable & Robinson Ltd 2006

ISBN 13: 978-1-84529-134-1
ISBN 10: 1-84529-134-4

Printed and bound in the EU

To Gwyn

Fiat justitia, ruat coelum
(Let justice be done though heaven fall)

Chapter One

'Mrs Bennett?'

Sue saw the uniform first, silver stripes on the shoulder. Her eyes went to the man's face and the look in his eyes. What she read there made muscles tighten in fear and she fought down the urge to run away and be sick. Dimly, she heard him introduce himself and his companion, and became aware of a policewoman.

'May we come in?' The voice was gruff, kindly.

Nodding, Sue led the way to the sitting room, taking comfort from the familiar things around her. The sergeant eased her into a chair and sat facing her. As though from a great distance his voice alternately whispered and boomed. She nodded mutely when asked if her husband was Colin Bennett. Gently, the big man told her what she had already guessed, the word 'accident' reverberating around her mind, pushing away what she did not want to accept.

Colin was dead.

Putting her key in the lock made Sue pause for a moment. There was a sense of finality this time. The coroner had decreed, the verdict was official. Today she had buried Colin. When she went into the flat there was no longer any chance he would look up, smiling, from his papers.

'I'll just put the kettle on, dear.' Her mother deposited handbag, gloves, and headed for the kitchen. 'It's all been so dreadful for you, but at least it's over – the public part, that is.'

There had been numbness since the first shock of the news. It had continued while others dealt with the aftermath of a sudden death. Sue had been calm, businesslike, carrying on with her work and grateful she used a computer terminal at home. There had been no need to go in to the *Journal* offices, see the pity on faces, feel warm clasps on her shoulder. Safely cocooned in the flat she could glance through her electronic mail and then, with a twitch of a button, it disappeared from view.

At the funeral, events remembered from other such occasions helped everyone through the stately rites. There had been grief, compassion, attempts to heal. Sue viewed it from afar as though she were in a vacuum which nothing could penetrate to wreck her precious composure.

It had been difficult at the Coroner's Court. She had never realized an inquest dredged up such private matters in public. She thought the police had been satisfied Colin's death was an accident. A fight had started on the crowded, rush-hour platform, people backing away from flying fists, possible knives. Colin had been jostled, knocked into space as the train for which he had waited zoomed towards his body on the line.

It was pure coincidence, the coroner had assured Sue. Had that been said to make up for the probing questions as to Colin's state of mind? They must have thought her too grief-stricken to guess they were checking the possibility of suicide.

Ending his life? Only the night before it happened, it was Colin who had suggested they start a family. It was such a precious moment between them, Sue refused to share it with officialdom, even if it could have scotched their imaginings. Now, there was no Colin, and there would be no baby.

'I'll go and change,' Sue told her father, taking with her the envelope an inspector had handed to her.

'Do you want me to see to that?' he asked gently.

8

'No – thanks, Dad. I just want to be on my own for a while.' She had hugged the envelope, holding all that had been returned to her from that last day.

Mr Lavin smiled and Sue saw how old he looked, lines dragging down his cheeks, white in his hair. Always he had seemed so young, vigorous, but seeing her suffer had hurt him too, and he looked his age.

'All right, Poppet. I'll get Mum to hold the tea till you're ready.'

Sue shut the bedroom door behind her and leaned against it, feeling hot tears ooze under her closed lids. She could get through as long as there was not too much sympathy. Her parents had been marvellous, rushing to her and prepared to stay as long as she needed them. She was grateful for their help, but it was time on her own she most wanted, time to let the horror, the misery wash over her. Sue knew she must come to terms with interminable days and even worse nights. She knew that, somehow, she must fight alone.

The dark suit, white shirt were quickly hung away, her black pumps kicked off into the depths of the wardrobe. Jeans and a warm sweater stopped the shivers which were beginning again, and she scuffed her feet into slip-ons, loose near her bed. Automatically, Sue reached for cleanser, rubbing it into her skin with unaccustomed firmness. Wiping it away she glanced at herself in the mirror. Her face was thinner, the skin purified by pain, shadows etched deeply under hazel eyes pale from so many tears. She looked her age too, Sue decided.

It did not matter now. Nothing did. A brush was wielded with a sudden gust of fury and futility, the resulting swing of dark hair gleaming with a brightness at odds with her mood.

Delaying her return to pity, Sue picked up the envelope from the bed and sat cross-legged, pouring the contents on to the duvet. Two handkerchieves, one unused, keys, coins. The watch she had given Colin two years ago was smashed beyond repair. He must have thrown up his arm to protect himself. The thought brought vivid images, bright with blood, and Sue recoiled, screaming silently with the agony of her imagination.

She forced herself to go on with her task and picked up the wallet. It was intact and Sue could guess what was in it, but everything must be checked. Credit cards, photos of the two of them, stamps, a couple of business cards from insurers, a folded piece of paper. Opening it, Sue saw a list of names and addresses in Colin's handwriting. Two were in London, ticks beside them. The rest stretched over the country, and there was a tick beside one in Bristol. Sue frowned. Colin had been to Bristol on a case only weeks before he – Sue's mind backed away from the reality, then she lifted her head.

'Before he died,' she said out loud.

There was a gentle knock at the door. Without thinking, Sue thrust the paper into the pocket of her jeans as her mother came into the room. Mrs Lavin looked thin in the dress she kept for funerals, black draining her of colour. 'Come and get your tea, Sue.' Her mother's face, once pretty, had softened with the years and her unhappiness until she was a tired, old woman.

'I'll just see to these first,' Sue told her, returning cards and banknotes to their places. When everything was back in the envelope, she stuffed it out of sight in the bedside drawer, trying to give her mother a reassuring smile as she did so. Later, Sue promised herself, she would go through it properly.

Usually, Sue drank her tea from a mug, but her mother had unearthed wedding-present china and a dainty tray was waiting.

'You pour, Mum.'

'If you want me to, darling.'

Scarcely had Mrs Lavin dealt with the milk jug before there was a ring at the doorbell.

'I'll go,' Mr Lavin said. 'You stay where you are, Sue. I'll try and persuade them to come back another time – you've seen enough people for today.'

10

'I'm fine, Dad,' she insisted, but it was to his disappearing back.

'When we've had tea, we'll finish loading up and get you away,' her mother promised.

Resigned, Sue nodded, sipping her tea and grateful for the heat as it fought the shaking inside her which seemed never to have stopped.

'Mr Skinner was most insistent he spoke to you.'

Her father was apologetic, and behind him a burly figure, the collar of his country-check shirt open, a brown woollen tie askew. Above the well-cut but battered sports jacket and corduroys was the large head and shaggy mane of a friend.

'Watty!' Sue ran to him, relieved to see solid normality. She hugged him hard.

The newcomer held her at a distance and scrutinized her features carefully. 'You're as skinny as my daughters. You've not been eating properly.'

'I do try,' her mother said.

Watty turned to the older woman. 'Watson Skinner, ma'am. A colleague of your daughter's – and, I hope, a friend.'

'I'm pleased to make your acquaintance, Mr Skinner. We've met so many friends of Sue's today.'

A quick frown conveyed Watty's mood. 'Only a demand from the Home Office kept me away from the funeral, Mrs Lavin. I thought a lot of young Colin. A good chap.' The soft Scots burr added warmth.

'It was a very good turn-out, Mr Skinner,' Mrs Lavin told him. 'So many from the courts. Colin seemed to have been very well regarded. I'm told several QCs were there to pay their respects.'

'Right and proper. Young Colin knew his job. As a defence solicitor, his briefs were always well prepared. Made the job a damned sight too easy for some of these silks.' Watty turned to Mr Lavin. 'I wouldn't have been surprised to see Colin appearing in court himself one of these days. It would have saved a helluva lot of expense for some poor devils.'

As her parents sighed with regret, Sue turned away, realizing afresh the emptiness in her core.

'Tea, Mr Skinner?' her mother invited.

'Or perhaps a scotch?' her father suggested with a smile.

'I could go a scotch,' Watty agreed, and when it was in his hand he caught hold of Sue's fingers, then raised his glass. 'To Colin. God bless the lad.'

Tears sprang, hot, gushing, and Sue sniffed.

'I gather you've been hard at work these last few days,' Watty said conversationally, helping Sue to behave normally. He squeezed her fingers. 'That terminal of yours has been damned near red-hot.' With his empty whisky glass he gestured to the computer tucked away in a corner of the room. 'Sam Haddleston tells me you've not only caught up, you've delivered a couple of articles to stir up trouble next week.'

'Do you work for the *Journal* too, Mr Skinner?'

'Watty, please.' He smiled at Sue's mother. The white in his hair made him look benevolent, and his green eyes were merry. 'Yes, I work there – or thereabouts, you might say. I'm usually out, chasing a story.'

'Watty's the chief crime reporter, Mum. He's got a nose for it.'

'I've read your work,' Mr Lavin told Watty. 'Gripping stuff.'

'Thank you. It's a sign of the times I've plenty to keep me occupied. I'm afraid, today, everyone's interested in the criminal – he's become major news.'

'You say "he", Mr Skinner. What about women?' Mrs Lavin asked. 'Surely they commit crimes too?'

'Not so many,' Watty said. 'Besides, a woman criminal gives a sense of chill which puts people off reading too much about them. It's the idea of woman as the universal mother-figure, I suppose. To think of her killing, maiming, it's just not acceptable. Stealing to feed her family – now, that's different. I can always get good copy out of that.'

'And the victims?' Mr Lavin asked quietly.

'Ah, the victims.' Watty twirled his glass, peering into its crystal depths as he did so. 'Mostly Joe Public thinks the poor devils were asking for it. Mugged in the street? What were they thinking of, being there? Shot while they shop? Well, if they didn't spend so much time and money on themselves, they wouldn't have been there in the first place, would they? No. I'm afraid these days a victim is there to be pitied, but the crook, he's there to be admired. They're the modern heroes.' The cynicism in the deep voice was scathing in its contempt.

'I think that's why I enjoy reading you, Mr Skinner,' Sue's father said gravely. 'You debunk the villains as being – just that. Evil.'

Watty looked hard at Mr Lavin, then smiled. 'Thank you.'

'Anything big on at the moment?' Sue wanted to know.

'Nothing much local. Keith's up in Liverpool, getting background on two murders.'

'Those gay men?' Mr Lavin frowned.

'Yep,' Watty agreed. 'See what I mean? They're as dead as dodos, but because they're gay, the vast majority of our readers will say "So what?" Yet they've got families who care, mothers, sisters, fathers.'

There was a stillness in the room, a silent mourning for homes where dreams had been lost, hope had died.

Watty turned to Sue and smiled. 'Now young lady, I hope you're going to have a break of some kind, a chance to rest? Joyce sends her love and tells me I have to make sure you get enough time off from the paper.'

'Thanks.' Sue was grateful for his concern.

'We're taking her back with us,' Mrs Lavin said.

'To see she gets some fresh air and home cooking,' her husband added, smiling at Sue.

'I'll be off then, and let you away.' Watty stood and Sue went to his hug, the mingled aromas of soap and pipe tobacco reassuringly familiar. 'Will there be someone to keep an eye on this place for you?'

'Yes, Pippa – a friend upstairs. She works from home too, so we usually keep tabs on each other.'

'And you'll be well locked up?' Watty insisted.

'Of course.' Sue smiled at him. 'Two Chubbs on the door, window locks and the burglar alarm. I'll have you know this flat doubles as Fort Knox.'

'I'm glad to hear it,' Watty told her solemnly. He made his farewells to her parents and was off.

As Mrs Lavin washed up the tea things and tidied the flat, Sue and her father finished loading the two cars.

'I don't see why we all couldn't have gone in our car,' her mother protested as Sue helped her into the passenger seat.

'Because I want to keep all four wheels on my wagon, thank you very much,' Sue insisted, 'and that's not likely to happen if I leave it unattended in Islington for too long. I'll lead, shall I, Dad?'

'Please,' he said, 'but not so fast I lose you at the first turning.'

After two days at home, Sue was ready to scream. Her parents were fine, but they had so many friends, each of whom must come with flowers and tell Sue how sorry they were, before urging her to tell them 'how it happened'. After that it was 'what about Colin's family?' and Sue must explain yet again about the sister in New Zealand. 'It's good for you to talk about it,' they told her, one by one, while her mother smiled encouragement with the tea pot and her father carried in the sherry decanter and glasses.

Sue had had her fill when the front doorbell rang again. Grabbing an anorak from the utility room, she sped out of the back door and went through the garden, scurrying away like a nocturnal animal as the sun rises. Back roads,

14

alleyways took her to the heath, the common land which ran between the houses and the railway line.

'Damn and blast,' she said to herself, as a familiar figure appeared, heading in her direction. A golden Labrador ran straight for Sue, greeting her like an old friend.

'Down, Hector!' its owner barked and the dog sat at Sue's feet. 'Sorry, m'dear. He's still a puppy.'

'He's no problem, Mrs Willoughby,' Sue said, bending to fondle the dog. She fervently wished it and its owner miles away. Mrs Willoughby had the loud voice and bullying manner associated with some of the best girls' schools, and was the terror of the bridge club.

'Glad to see you getting out, m'dear. You've been working too hard.'

Sue looked up in surprise, and met frank concern in the blue eyes under fierce brows and grizzled, cropped hair.

'Oh, yes, I read your pieces. Very good, if I may say so. I always liked your science articles, but when you've doubled up as medical correspondent, I seem to understand the damned stuff much better. I don't hold with doctors keeping everything secret and pretending they know all the answers. It's best for patients to know the truth – however hard. Still, you must pace yourself, you know.' She cleared her throat. 'I was damned sorry to hear about your husband. Jolly bad luck.'

Somehow, Mrs Willoughby's brusque manner conveyed real feeling.

'It's true what they say about time, m'dear,' she went on, 'it does help. What's so bloody impossible is getting through it until it's done its job. You just have to keep your body and your mind busy. How? Well, that's up to you. But it must be you that decides, m'dear. It's you that has to endure.'

The urgency in her voice made Sue aware Mrs Willoughby had been an inhabitant of the icy hollow in which she now found herself. 'People seem to queue at the door to tell me what to do,' she said ruefully.

'I know, m'dear. They can only reach you when you're

vulnerable, so get yourself occupied away from them. Now, with me it was gardening. I'd nursed my husband, poor darling, and when it was over, I gardened. God, how I did for that blasted couch grass! But it's worse for you – the suddenness. At least I had time to say goodbye. Well, I'll be off. Hector!' The dog ran to heel and Mrs Willoughby turned to Sue. 'Remember, m'dear. Do it your way.'

Strangely comforted, Sue walked on, returning home hungry for the first time in days. In the kitchen which had seen her grow from baby to widow she made herself a sandwich, eating it as she walked about, handling her mother's treasures and being flooded with memories of a carefree childhood.

'There you are, dear. I didn't hear you come in.' Mrs Lavin was comfortable in a navy wool skirt, the collar of her blue-and-white checked shirt standing up in a touch of colour against the darkness of her navy sweater. She filled the kettle and switched it on. 'Tea? Or sherry? Mrs Stroat's in the sitting room. She's been here a while, waiting for you to come home.' Her mother spoke carefully, not look-ing at Sue.

'I'd rather the vicar had come – not sent his wife. He's nothing like as nosey.' Sue frowned, rebellious.

'She's only trying to do what she thinks is best. You finish your sandwich and then come through. I'll keep her busy – it'll shorten the time you have to talk to her. There's cherry cake in the tin.' Mrs Lavin picked up the tea tray and marched into battle.

Sue found the cake, cut herself a slice and sat eating it slowly, remembering days when she returned from school and sat at the same table, her hopes, ambitions in full flood.

'God, that woman!' Mr Lavin exploded as he shut the kitchen door behind him. 'The KGB have nothing on her.'

'What's she been up to?'

'Trying to find out what golden handshake bank

16

employees get when they're made redundant. Thank God I retired years ago and know nothing.'

Sue smiled up at her father, his flare of temper loosening his white curls, making them dance. 'He's so nice – Mr Stroat,' she said while she watched her father furiously tidy mugs on a stand. 'He loves his job, but she sits looking all pathetic and doing her "you lucky people don't know what it's like being poor".' Sue became intent on eating the cherries she had saved for last and did not see the gleam of hope in her father's eyes as he heard the beginnings of healing anger.

'Poor?' Mr Lavin laughed.

'The clergy don't get paid much. Nice houses, yes,' Sue insisted between nibbles.

'But there are always bequests,' Mr Lavin said, smiling and tapping the side of his nose.

'What do you mean, Dad?'

Mr Lavin drew the cake tin towards him and cut a slice of cake. If Sue was prepared to be diverted, he would do his best.

'Mrs Stroat is very good with little old ladies who are a bit short on family,' Mr Lavin explained. 'Her social work, she calls it.'

'So?' Sue was prepared to listen and not hurry to the sitting room.

'She's only interested in the ones with cash tucked away, then it's simply a case of water wearing away stone. She keeps telling the housebound old biddies how lucky they are to have so much, then sends along poor old Norman. He's a genuinely nice chap with a real calling for the church. The old ladies take to him, and hey presto, when they die, it's "X hundreds or thousands to the dear vicar and his wife who have been so good to me in my last days".'

Sue tipped her head on one side, the finger which had been stirring crumbs on her plate still. 'And?'

'Over the years I reckon it's getting on for eighty thousand pounds, at least.'

17

She sat up startled. 'You're joking!'

'No. The old boy always gives what he can to the church, but Mrs Stroat hangs on to hers like grim death. I suppose she reckons she's earned it.'

'The old cow!'

'Come on, Sue, it's for her old age – and being the kind of person she is, it'll be a lonely one. She's got no friends.'

'It's immoral,' she protested.

'It's happening all the time.'

Mr Lavin brushed his fingers free of crumbs. Sue's interest had been aroused and if he could stop her thinking of her loss for a little longer, it was well worth a bit of slander.

'Do you remember Great-aunt Kate?'

'Vaguely. We used to go and see her in Llandudno.'

'Well, she had a doctor who worked like Mrs Stroat. There were a lot of elderly people on their own up there, and he was keen on antiques. He had a very effective system when he was doing a home visit. "Mrs So-and-so, it's a pleasure to visit you. You cheer up my very dull day – and that picture of yours, charming. A Stubbs, do you think? Delightful." This was repeated once a week while he doled out prescriptions to keep the old girl happy and when the will was read it was "to dear Doctor Whatsit, the picture he always admired, from a grateful patient". When the "dear doctor" retired, it was to a house stuffed with a fortune in antiques for which he hadn't paid a penny. No, I tell a lie – ninety pounds, actually.'

Sue laughed. 'Come on, Dad.'

'It's true. He kept on to Aunt Kate about a desk she had. She was going to move into a small flat and there would have been no room for it, so he buttered her up good and proper, expecting her to hand it over.'

'I can't imagine it worked with Aunt Kate.' Sue's memories were of a most formidable little lady.

'It didn't. She offered to sell it to him for a hundred pounds, what she'd have got on a bad day at auction.'

'You said ninety pounds?'

'He haggled.'

It was with the remains of a smile that Sue went into the sitting room and the cloying sympathy of Mrs Stroat. At first, all went well. Sue made the correct responses and sat stiffly, her mother a trifle anxious when she saw her daughter's expression. The younger woman was courteous, but it became increasingly difficult to go on being polite as the vicar's wife probed.

'A terrible accident, Sue. I understand it was the result of a fight. Your dear husband wasn't involved, surely?'

Sue looked into the soft face, with its full, unpainted mouth and heavy-lidded eyes. 'No, not at all. He was some distance away but the platform was crowded.'

Mrs Stroat went on unheard as Sue remembered a face from the inquest. She could not remember if it was that of a policeman or someone from London Transport. It was the expression she could see again, doubt in the frown. What had been the question? 'From the security video, was Mr Bennett seen to have been knocked off the platform because of the fighting?' Why should she think of that now?

'. . . still, a young woman like you, there will be young men queuing up.' Mrs Stroat sounded smugly confident.

Sue returned to the present, struggling to regain the thread of the visitor's conversation. With a shock, she realized the drift of the woman's words.

What had been mild irritation began to build into fury. Sue held on to her control. She had endured so much these last weeks, this dreadful woman must not be the one to break her.

'It's only two days since my husband was buried, Mrs Stroat. He's still real to me.' Sue's voice tinkled with splinters of ice and Mrs Lavin leaned forward anxiously. 'Your idea that I might replace him —'

'My dear! Of course not! How stupid of me to have made it seem so. No, I was merely trying to say that a pretty girl like you, with your good job, and now the

19

money your husband will have left you, well, you'll be a catch, there's no doubt of it. You have to watch out for the kind of man who'll try to ensnare you while you're at a low ebb. I mean, your late husband was a solicitor. He'll have been thorough with insurances, things like that. I'm sure he's left you well provided for?'

Sue looked at the older woman. The heavy lids had lifted and little eyes, bright as polished granite, demanded an answer. Sue's temper flared. Her breathing was becoming shallow, air expelled from flaring nostrils.

'More tea, Mrs Stroat?' Mrs Lavin intervened, the request an order. 'Sue? More tea for you?'

There was an old familiarity to the tone of her mother's voice and Sue responded to the authority, sinking back in her chair, her jaw clenched tightly. The awkward silence was disturbed by the telephone ringing in the hall.

Not long after the sound stopped, Mr Lavin came into the sitting room. 'Sue. For you. Pippa. Do you want to take it?'

With a lithe movement Sue was out of her chair and through the door, its closure only just short of a slam.

'Pippa.'

'Is anything wrong? You sound a bit funny.'

'So would you if you'd had to put up with the most God-awful bitch.'

'I'm sorry. I thought you'd be better off at home.'

'So did I. I forgot how much it's possible to enjoy being anonymous in London. Still, how about you? Everything OK?'

There was a pause, then Pippa spoke slowly. 'I'm not sure. I went into the flat on Saturday to see to your mail. There's nothing special, unless you want catalogues for double glazing and conservatories sent on?'

'No, thank you. They're not on my list of priorities at the moment.'

'I didn't go in yesterday as there was no post, and I've only just been in today. There are a couple of letters that look official, and I was going to readdress them, but –'

20

'Pippa, what is it?'

'Sue, I know it sounds stupid: I've got absolutely no reason for saying it but I think someone's been in your flat.'

Leaving behind hasty goodbyes and an excuse that a big story was about to break, Sue was soon back in London. Pippa was watching for her and the two women met at the door of Sue's flat.

'I feel silly, bringing you all this way, and maybe for nothing.'

'Nonsense,' Sue said briskly. 'The one thing you're not is silly.'

'But there's no reason.'

'I'm supposed to be the scientist,' Sue grinned, 'you're the artistic one.' She looked at the locks for signs of scratches, forced entry. Finding none, she used her two Chubb keys to unlock the door. 'So,' she asked Pippa when they stood in the small hall, the alarm switched off, 'something must – have made you wonder. What was it?'

Pippa frowned. She was big-boned, lean, her long fair hair caught back with a batik scarf. Like Sue she wore jeans and a sweater, Pippa's bright with swirling colour.

'It was when I first came in. Something about the hall.' She sniffed. 'That was it! It was a smell.'

'Nice? Nasty?'

'Male. Definitely male.' Pippa closed her eyes, trying to remember, then opened them wide again. 'Aftershave. The sort I've smelt before, but never here, and certainly not on Saturday.'

'So,' Sue said reflectively, 'a man has been in here. Firstly why?' She led the way to the sitting room which appeared to have been untouched, then the bedroom, bathroom, kitchen. 'Nothing seems to have been moved.'

Pippa was checking the shelves of the sitting room. 'All your silver bits are intact. That print Colin paid the earth for is still on the wall. Money?'

'Only the pot in the hall, for parking, or charity collectors.' Sue lifted the coins in the small pot and let them fall from her fingers. 'It feels the same. Besides, if they were going to take any, why not the lot?'

'I've dragged you away for nothing,' Pippa said. 'I'm sorry, Sue. You needed all the rest you could get.'

'Even if no one got in, you did me a favour.'

'How come?'

Sue described the antics of Mrs Stroat, Pippa gasping with horror that anyone could be quite so insensitive.

'I think we could both do with coffee.'

Sue went into the kitchen and switched on the central heating. Beans were poured into the grinder and she turned it sharply, lips pursed, chin firm. With great care she measured the ground coffee into the cafetière. The sharp aroma heartened the two women.

'Another thing,' Sue said, puzzled. 'If a man got in, how? You and I are the only ones with keys. Then they'd have to know about the alarm.'

'Unless I'd forgotten to switch it back on.'

'Had you?'

'I thought I did, but maybe –' Pippa stopped, irresolute.

With her build and colouring Pippa had the air of a sleepy lioness, but Sue knew the artist's eye was sharp, the mind behind it retaining every detail, however small.

'If you thought you did, then I believe you. To be this clever, they'd manage an alarm, no problem.'

With the coffee poured, Sue led the way into the sitting room. With gas flames curling round imitation coals, the room welcomed, warmed. She curled in the corner of the couch while Pippa sat on the floor, her back against the armchair. The heat from the mugs helped to induce a sense of release.

'Will you ring the police?' Pippa asked.

'I don't know. It seems pointless.' Sue stood up, restless. 'I'll have another look round.' In the bedroom she sat at her dressing-table. Unwilling to look at herself and feel pity for the widow she would see there, her eyes used the mirror to see her bedroom in reverse. As she wondered how she could become used to living in it on her own, Sue stiffened. There was something odd about her bedside table. Frowning, she tried to remember when she had last touched it.

It was hard to go back into that dark abyss. Sue pushed her mind, sluggish as it was, against memories solid with despair. A glimmer of light appeared. Tea. She could hear china clinking in her memory, feel brown paper between her fingers. Of course! The envelope with Colin's effects. She had put it in the drawer in a hurry and it had jammed. Too preoccupied to fiddle with the drawer, she had left it open a fraction, the corner of the envelope protruding.

Sue turned her head slowly, reluctant to look. The drawer was closed properly.

'Pippa.'

Pippa ambled in.

'When you've been in for the mail, did you ever come in here?'

Pippa shook her head. 'No. Why?'

'I'm sure I left this drawer open a fraction.'

'Perhaps you closed it before you left.'

Sue shook her head. 'No. Dad hurried us away.' She sat on the bed and took a deep breath before she pulled out the drawer.

The envelope had gone.

Chapter Two

'And you're quite sure you did not take the envelope away with you?'

The young policeman was tired, bored with the trivia of what was for him a very petty crime.

'Quite sure.' Sue was adamant, and a little annoyed.

'No one else could have taken it on your behalf? You did say you left last Friday with your parents.' The suggestion hung in the air. Mummy and Daddy hen protecting their chick.

'No,' Sue said firmly 'It was here when I left, and gone when I returned.'

'Your friend upstairs in Flat 4,' he consulted his notes, 'Ms Pippa Endacott. Could she have moved the envelope?'

'She did not.'

They might be very pleasant people in their own time, the two men allocated to the reported crime, smart in dark grey suits and stylish ties, but Sue was not at all sure they thought she had been robbed.

'We'll make a note of it, madam. Can you tell us what was in the envelope?'

'Two handkerchieves, one unused. A broken watch. Coins.' It was becoming an automatic list.

'How much?' the note-taker wanted to know, while the other, taller and older, walked round the room, examining the windows.

'I didn't count it. A couple of pounds in silver, I would guess.'

It was solemnly entered. 'Anything else?'

'Keys on a ring. With a tab of a bull's head.' Unbidden tears started in Sue's eyes. Colin had been a Pisces, she a Taurean.

'Ah, keys. For the front door? That could explain the break-in.'

'For heaven's sake! You're not suggesting the burglar unlocked the door with keys he'd not yet stolen?'

'No, madam. Of course not,' the younger CID man said hastily while his sergeant turned from the window and smiled at his discomfiture. 'Was there anything else?'

'A wallet,' Sue said, trying to be patient. 'It had about forty pounds in notes, credit cards –'

'Could they be used?' It was the senior man, taking an interest at last.

'No,' Sue assured him. 'My father stopped all Colin's cards as soon as he heard the news he had been killed. He's a retired bank manager, so he understood the need for speed.'

'Oh, he was a bank manager.' The two men smiled at each other. 'Very useful for you,' the sergeant told her.

The sergeant was tall, rangy, smelling of stale tobacco and lunchtime beer. 'Are all your husband's other papers intact? He was a solicitor, I believe? Farnham, Welburn and Bennett. They do a lot of criminal work. Perhaps one of his former clients got in to take away embarrassing files.'

'Not as far as I know. Colin's briefcase went back to his office immediately, because of ongoing cases. Some papers, he kept here. One of the other partners is coming tonight to sort them, but there's no way I'd know if any had gone.'

'You'll give us a ring if you can add to the list of stolen goods?'

Sue nodded.

'It's strange, there being no sign of forced entry. Almost as though someone had a key, or you just thought you'd put the envelope in the drawer,' the sergeant suggested.

Sue hated being patronized and the tall policeman's smooth manner irritated her. 'Sergeant. Just because I have

25

been deprived of my husband, I have not suddenly become moronic.'

'Of course not, Mrs Bennett,' he hastened to assure her, 'far from it.' He nodded to the terminal near the window. 'Did your husband use that?'

'No. Never. It's one I use for my work, so it's linked in to the *Journal*.'

'And no newspaper would like a solicitor having access to their files, would they?'

'It never arose.'

'That's the only computer in here?'

Sue hesitated for a split second. 'Yes,' she said, truthfully.

After the men had gone, promising to make inquiries, Sue emptied the boot of her car. Why had she not been prepared to tell them about the lap-top computer she kept with her always? Was it because Colin sometimes did use it, and if he had left any memos she wanted to be the first to see them?

Sue busied herself making the flat look presentable. Fortunately many of the flowers were still fresh, and it calmed her to sort and arrange the blooms, their fragrances good company. If Bill Farnham was coming, she wanted everything to look its best. He and his wife lived in a great deal of Georgian splendour in Buckinghamshire. It would not do for him to pity the junior partner's widow in her Islington flat.

The bell rang and Sue was quickly at the door, trying to force a relaxed smile from stiff muscles. Instead of Bill Farnham's silver-haired urbanity it was Colin's friend Ken Miller, looking tired and drawn after a day in court.

'Sorry, it's me, Sue. Bill couldn't make it. His wife's in the Eaton Square flat for the night, and she's crooked her little finger. Some big do at Covent Garden.'

Sue grinned. 'Bill never takes chances when it comes to Lady Jane's money.' She led the way into the sitting room.

Ken stood for a moment, absorbing the low couches, gentle lighting, restful colours. The smell of fresh coffee was just defeating the crispness of greenery, flowers. 'This is nice.'

Sue was aware of wistfulness in his voice. 'Thank you. I'm sorry you've got extra work tonight. You could have done with some time off. I know it's you who has been landed with all Colin's cases.'

Ken became brisk, stripping off his overcoat and running a hand through thick dark hair springing with an unruly life of its own. 'Let's have those papers, then. And some of that coffee wouldn't go amiss.' The smile started in his eyes, then lightened his face.

'Have you eaten?'

'Not yet. I'll grab a take-away on the way home.'

'No you will not. My mother's stocked my freezer to bursting. You'll be doing me a favour if you help me eat some of it. A whisky while I get the files?'

He groaned. 'I'm being spoilt. Carry on.'

When Sue appeared from the kitchen with his meal on a tray Ken was sitting in his shirt sleeves, orderly piles of paper and folders around him on the couch.

'How's it going?' she asked as she settled the tray on a low table in front of him.

'Very straightforward, on the whole. That's the private stuff.' He pointed to a heap on the floor by her feet. 'You may want to go through it yourself, one day. The rest I can take to the office. There are letters and notes there which should be with this file, but I expect they're in Colin's desk at the office. His secretary can help with that.'

'Good. Now eat.'

'Aren't you joining me?'

'I'm not very hungry.'

'Go on. I feel embarrassed eating on my own.'

Sue smiled. 'I'll get something. Do you want some wine?'

'Better not. I'm driving, and I've already had that large whisky. Coffee would be great.'

They ate in companionable silence.

'Are you as good a cook as your mother?'

Sue laughed. 'Not quite, but she did make sure I could feed myself properly before I left home.'

He sighed. 'And then some. I don't know when I've had a home-cooked meal like that.' For a moment his face was dark, brooding.

'Colin told me about your wife. I'm sorry.'

'Knowing Colin, it would have been a sanitized version.'

'He said you'd divorced after you left the police, and that you were still a little bitter about it.'

'Good old Colin,' Ken said, with affection, 'he'd make the best of anyone's motives.' He looked at Sue from dark eyes under level brows. 'When I was invalided out of the job, I got some compensation. I wanted to invest it in training as a solicitor. I already had a law degree, thanks to the great Metropolitan Police, and it would not have taken too long. Unfortunately Nicola, my wife, had other ideas. She thought she deserved the money spent on her.'

Sue waited while unpleasant memories flooded him.

'She got good legal advice,' Ken said at last, 'and divorced me as quickly as she could, claiming half the money. I struck a deal. She could have the lot, as long as that was the end of any financial set-up between us. No one could have signed more quickly. There'd been a boy-friend in the offing, long before I got shot at, and he helped her spend it. Last I heard, it had all gone – and so had he. Serve her right.'

'No children?'

'No, thank God. Or rather, thanks to Nicola. Her figure, you see. Too important.'

Sue was puzzled. 'How did you come to marry?'

Ken laughed. 'When you're a young copper, and you spend all your days and nights cleaning up London's muck, you're easily tempted to go home to something beautiful. The one thing about Nicola, she was a stunner.'

There was silence in the room, Ken lost in his thoughts. He stirred himself. 'No good thinking of what's gone.' He realized what he had said and was penitent. 'Oh Sue, I'm sorry. I didn't mean –'

'It's all right,' she smiled. 'It's been good talking to you, and cooking for you. I've had an awful job keeping the freezer door closed. Now it does.'

'Put these away somewhere safe.' Ken handed Sue the pile of papers he had said were private. 'Keep them a while, then read them,' he advised. 'Now, Bill Farnham should be off the hook in the daytime, and he's insisted on seeing to Colin's estate, so anything you need to know, Bill's secretary –'

'Judith?'

'Yes,' he grinned, 'it's still Judith. She'll let you know when you can see the lord of all he surveys.'

Sue cleared away the supper things, finding pleasure in restoring the flat to neatness. She went to her bedroom, putting away the clothes she had thrown hurriedly into cases before running away from Mrs Stroat. There seemed to be a large pile needing washing, and she carried the accumulated jeans, undies, shirts, to the kitchen. Methodically Sue checked the pockets, tissues discarded in the waste bin, odd coins on to the counter. In a jeans pocket she found the sheet of paper with the list Colin had made. It was all she had left of the contents of the envelope, and suddenly precious. She smoothed it, reading out loud the names and addresses as though they were a litany.

With the paper folded again and safe in a zippered section of her handbag, Sue stuffed her washing machine and switched it on. The coins she was carrying to the hall for the little pot when the phone rang. It was her mother, determinedly cheerful. Sue was able to reassure her that everything was fine, one helping of the beef and mushroom casserole had gone to a good home, that she would soon be in bed, ready for a busy day at the *Journal* tomorrow.

Sue was cleaning her teeth when the phone rang again. It was Pippa.

'I know it's late, but I wanted to make sure you were all right.'

'I'm OK. I thought an early night might be a good idea.'

'Fancy a nightcap?'

'I'm in pyjamas,' Sue laughed.

'So – I'll come down. One minute, thirty seconds.'

True to her word, Pippa rang the bell on time. In one hand she had a jar of coffee, in the other a bottle of Baileys.

'De-caffeinated,' Pippa said, waving the jar. 'It'll help us sleep. I've been trying to make Dennis Dormouse look as though he could defend his friends the field mice by taking on Freddy Ferret – and that's not easy.'

Sue chuckled. Pippa illustrated a series of children's books and it was obvious she had been hard at work. Her fair hair was wispy from having paint brushes thrust in, and there was a smudge of light green paint high on one cheekbone.

'I need this as much as you do,' Pippa told Sue, waving the supplies she had brought. 'You go and get your feet up, I'll make the coffee.'

It was companionable in the warm room. Sue stretched out on the couch while Pippa lay on the floor, cushions under her head and feet.

'How was the Great I Am?' Pippa wanted to know.

'He didn't come. It was Ken Miller.'

'The ex-cop? He's dishy.'

Pippa lived alone from choice, but Sue had been aware that at the infrequent parties she and Colin had given, Pippa and Ken migrated towards each other. Neither was in a hurry to repeat past mistakes. Their friendship was loosely based, flexible, at least it appeared so to a casual observer.

Sue kept her expression bland. 'He's still anti-woman apparently.'

Pippa digested the opinion. 'Did he find anything missing from Colin's papers?'

'No,' Sue said slowly. 'Well, yes.'

Pippa drank deeply from her mug. 'Which?'

'There's some bumpf he expected to find in the files here. It's probably in the office somewhere.'

'I see. I would have thought all Colin's paperwork there had already been dealt with.' Pippa gazed at the ceiling. She turned towards Sue, lifting herself on to an elbow. 'Strange, these little mysteries, if Colin's death was the accident the coroner insisted it was.'

It was Sue's turn to inspect the ceiling.

'There's been something niggling you,' Pippa said quietly. 'What is it?'

In a calm voice, Sue spoke of the man's face at the inquest. 'It's maddening. I can't remember who it was.'

'Get hold of the transcript,' Pippa advised, before pulling herself erect and taking the mugs back to the kitchen for a refill.

'Who do you ask?' Sue wanted to know.

'The *Journal*'s got a legal department, hasn't it? Put them on to it.'

'It seems so cold-blooded, wanting to know all the details.'

'But you don't,' Pippa called from the kitchen. She came back to Sue and handed her a steaming mug. 'Only one.'

'Mmm.' Sue sipped, and the hot liquid eased the kernel of coldness. 'If I find the man, and he tells me he doesn't think Colin's death was an accident . . .' Her voice tailed off into silence.

'And it wasn't suicide.'

'No. That's one thing I am sure about.'

Pippa's eyes met Sue's. 'It only leaves one possibility.'

'I suppose I realized that when I knew the flat had been burgled so professionally – but why?' Sue begged.

'One of his clients?'

Sue shook her head, Pippa's answer amplified by a

31

resolute swing of dark silkiness. 'No. He did well by them. They'd want him alive.'

'Then who?'

'If I can find out why, I'll know who,' Sue said, her voice strong.

'You?' Pippa was surprised.

'Why not? Who else really cares enough?'

Pippa was concerned. 'It could be risky.'

'I've already lost what really mattered.'

Both sipped their coffee, denying each other their thoughts for a moment.

'Do you think you should be here on your own?' Pippa asked.

'In case someone comes back? There's no point. They got all they came for.'

'It wasn't that, so much as . . .'

'I know,' Sue said. 'It's the first night I'll have spent on my own since Colin was killed.'

'I can stay, if it would help.'

Sue sat up, pink flushing her cheeks. 'No, Pippa. Thank you – but no. I've got to do it, and don't worry. I'll be fine.'

It was difficult to be so sure when Pippa had gone and Sue lay alone in the big bed. She lay back and cradled Colin's pillow, trying to sleep.

It was a very long night.

Next morning, Sue decided she must have dozed off now and again, but it was hard to remember clearly. Wintry sunshine streamed through the windows on to a bed, half of which was smooth. Before going to shower and dress, Sue laid her cheek against Colin's pillow, as though to wish him good morning. Her skin met dampness.

Hurrying to the bathroom, she was filled with resolution. Whatever it took, she would find who had caused Colin's death, accident or not. They would pay.

*　　*　　*

When Sue went in to the *Journa*‍
to believe so much time ha
work. Everyone she met
only able to spare seconds
to convey their concern for

Settling at a desk she tap
checked requests for articles.
waiting. After looking up her
on BSE in cows and humans for Sa
ing his war against German politicia
paragraphs on Crohn's disease for C
legal department. Something to do with
ter. Sue smiled to herself as she typed a
Clive could see to getting it translated into l
was enough.

A copy of the *New Scientist* bumped down
desk, courtesy of a spotty girl with an infectious
picked up the magazine, sniffing the freshness of
edition as she riffled the pages, then began to read. I
a relief to sit amongst the voices, phones, computers
read, sending her mind away from the everyday wor
which was demanding so much of her courage.

Peace did not last long. A shrill voice pierced her concentration, and Sue looked up to see Kate Jeffries arguing
with Cary Mitchell, the gossip columnist. It was a daily
ritual and Sue picked up her bag and the *New Scientist*,
determined to be on her way before Kate's impossibly red
coiffeur headed in her direction. To be smothered in clouds
of Diorissima and Turkish cigarette smoke while being
drained of every emotion and idea one possessed, was not
Sue's idea of being at work for the day.

''Bye Kate,' she left behind her as she hurried out. 'Got
to get to the London Hospital and see Gerry.' She waved
the magazine in her hand like a shield. 'Fantastic article –
he'll have the background. I want to pick his brains.'

Why had she decided to go to Whitechapel, Sue wondered? It was just as easy to pick up the phone. Come to

d better ring Gerry and be sure he could make
hurried to her parking slot.

g shut her mobile phone, Sue started the car and
out in a traffic stream which would take her to
hapel Road and the hospital. Gerry was a medical
ist, middle-aged, kindly. He was an inspired cook
with his partner, one of the hospital's consultants,
dinner parties most of Wapping's finest would have
en their eye teeth to attend. Colin and Sue had been
ular guests in the immaculate and spacious flat Gerry
d Richard had made their home.
Sue did not have long to wait in reception. Gerry
appeared, his white coat exchanged for a jacket and warm
ulster.

'Let's walk,' he suggested, taking Sue's arm.

The cold, fresh air stimulated them to a brisk pace. As
they headed away from the hospital, Gerry gave Sue the
background to the article which had intrigued her, spicing
his information with gossipy comments.

'It's nice we're early,' he said as they neared the pub he
had suggested. 'We can get a quiet corner.'

In the warm hospitality of the bar, Sue was aware of
Gerry's keen scrutiny, but it was caring, not intrusive.

'You order,' she told him. 'It's on the *Journal*.'

'How very kind of them. Next time, let's make it the
Savoy.'

Gerry continued to entertain Sue with chat from the
laboratories. When the waiter appeared with their food,
Gerry was in the middle of describing the antics of a lady
chemist at a conference in Luxembourg.

'Gerry,' Sue protested, 'you can't mean she –'

'My dear,' he insisted, his expression solemn, his eyes
amused, 'she did. Twice.'

They settled to their meal, Sue realizing Gerry had
found a pub with a first-rate chef.

'A little fatty for me,' he decided of the pork ribs coated

34

with a mild mustard before being dipped in beaten egg, breadcrumbs, and fried. 'Never mind, they're delicious,' he added, delicately forking crisp lettuce. 'Just remember to eat a handful of walnuts every day to help lower your cholesterol.'

Sue laughed, happy in the alcoved peace away from the lunchtime noisiness. 'I believe you.'

'You should. It works.'

'You've tested it?'

'Naturally. Mind you it was ten weeks before the cholesterol level plateaued out. Best to say three months, but it was a nine per cent drop in my case, thirteen in Richard's.'

'You did daily blood tests for three months?'

'Hardly vampire stuff, dear.' Gerry permitted himself a smile. 'One drop's enough, you know that.'

'I bet you took extra iron while you were doing it.'

'No. Afterwards, we did.' He laid his cutlery neatly together on his plate and wiped his lips with the red paper napkin. Behind the gleaming gold-framed glasses, his eyes were gentle. 'So, Sue. Why did you really come?'

Gerry had always been devastatingly intuitive, and Sue hesitated before she spoke. 'I don't know. It seemed natural to come to you. There was the article, of course, and yet – I suppose it's because of the list.'

Sue took the paper from her handbag and handed it to Gerry. 'I've not shown this to anyone else.'

Gerry took the list and read it slowly, his cheeks a little pink with the compliment he had been paid.

'I see the first on the list, this Porter person, lives in Burwell Close. That's near here. You go down New Road and Cannon Street, turning into Cable Street. A left down by Shadwell tube station and your A to Z will get you the rest of the way.'

He turned the sheet over. 'What do these letters mean? Any idea?'

Sue frowned. 'I've never noticed them.'

Heads together they tried to decipher marks made almost illegible by being rubbed on the crease.

'I think it's P – no, R perhaps. R C M L,' Gerry decided.

She agreed. 'The R is very shaky. Being in my jeans pocket probably did that,' she said ruefully.

'It doesn't matter what it is, Sue. You keep it safe.'

The scrap of paper had mattered enough to Colin to have been kept in his wallet. Now it was important to Sue as a relic, an icon.

'I've a feeling the ticks meant Colin had been to see them.' She explained about the visit to Bristol.

'Then go and begin your pilgrimage, Sue. Because that's what it is,' Gerry said as he rose.

She looked up, startled.

'It'll help. Believe me. It will help.'

There had been talk in the past of a former partner of Gerry's, dead after a gay-bashing gang attacked him in the street. Was that why she had sought out the humane man? Because he, too, had been close to someone selected for a kill and would know what she was suffering.

Table-seeking customers invaded their quiet corner and Sue rose, Gerry making sure she was warmly wrapped before they faced the outdoor chill. Walking back towards the hospital, Gerry talked of the work Richard and he were having done in the flat.

'You must see it, Sue. Come soon.'

They were at her car. 'Thanks, Gerry.'

He squeezed her shoulder and hurried back to his work.

The woman who opened the door was painfully thin, her clothes chosen for warmth, not style. She must have been pretty when she was young, Sue decided. 'Mrs Porter?'

'Yes.' The tone was abrupt, unfriendly, the pale blue eyes suspicious.

'My name's Bennett. Sue Bennett. I know this may

sound strange, but did my husband Colin Bennett come to see you?'

'What if he did?'

Sue felt a sense of relief. 'Please, could I talk to you about it?'

Mrs Porter hesitated. 'Why don't you ask him?'

'I can't,' Sue said quietly. 'He died. Not quite three weeks ago.'

Compassion drove out the last caution. 'Come in.'

Sue was ushered into a tiny sitting room.

'I'll put the kettle on,' Mrs Porter said after she had persuaded Sue to sit on the sofa.

Sue leaned back against crushed raspberry dralon and looked around her. Unlined pink curtains framed a view of the street. The carpet was beige, and there was a fluffy pink mat alongside gleaming hearth tiles where a small electric fire did battle with the cold. Everything was so clean and neat. Too neat? Photographs were a disciplined array across the mantel. Sue leaned forward to look. Each one was of a mother, father, small daughter, a family moment of happiness frozen in time. Sue frowned, puzzled. There was no sense of family in the room.

Mrs Porter came back with a tray. While the kettle had been heating, she had taken the time to brush her hair and find a lipstick, looking years younger as a result.

Hot tea helped both women.

'Your husband. How did it happen?' Mrs Porter wanted to know. 'Had he been ill long?'

Sue explained the fight, the fall.

Mrs Porter's features crumpled in distress. 'But that was terrible for you – sudden, like that. That's when it's worst. It's the shock does it. Nothing in you works properly. You cry and then you find yourself wanting to scream like a loony. People you love, you just can't bear them near you.'

Sue thought of her parents insisting on trying to shield her from more hurt. It had been with a sense of relief mixed with guilt that she had driven back to London, escaping them.

Mrs Porter was wringing her hands as if to squeeze her misery out of them. 'At least you couldn't blame yourself, like I do.' The words were violent, bitter.

'What happened?'

'Karen – my little girl. It was all my fault. She wanted to go out and play with her friends. I let her go. If I hadn't –' Hands covered the thin face. They hid the distress, the cascading tears.

'I'm sorry. To come here and bring it all back. I didn't know.'

With an effort Mrs Porter stopped crying, wiping her face. 'No. I'm sorry. You've got enough to get on with.'

Sue realized the woman was not much older than herself. It was the strain, the unhappiness which had drawn myriad fine lines in the fair skin.

'It's just that I found your address amongst Colin's things,' Sue explained. 'I thought he had come here, and I wanted . . .' The right words would not come. 'I don't know what I wanted,' she confessed lamely.

'To feel him close.' Mrs Porter nodded. 'I did the same after Karen died. I kept going to her school and watching the children play. I'd even go down the park and watch them on the swings.'

'How old was she, when . . .?'

'Seven, nearly eight. I'd already got her present for her next birthday Do you want to see it?'

Sue nodded and Mrs Porter hurried from the room, returning with a tiny shell suit, bright with cyclamen and jade. 'Like it?'

'It's lovely.' Sue fingered the material and smiled her approval. 'What did Colin talk about?'

'Karen dying. The trial.'

'Trial?'

'Oh, yes. Karen was murdered, Mrs Bennett, didn't you know?'

Sue felt shock hit like a physical blow. 'I'm so sorry,

38

I had no idea.' She sought for words to ease the moment, but felt only inadequacy. 'I should never have come like this.' As she said the words, Sue wondered why she was there, what significance this destroyed family had for Colin. Had Karen, like Colin, been selected for a kill?

'Never mind, the police got him – the beast who took her away from us. Life, he got, the judge said, but you know what that means these days. Out again and another child dies.' Mrs Porter took back the shell suit and hugged it to her. 'Gary, my husband, he couldn't take it. He went off with another woman. He's got a new baby now.'

'You didn't want another baby?'

'No! Not while that – creature still lived. His kind think we just have babies for them to use. Was I supposed to go through all that again – and have him come back when she was seven? Still,' she smiled grimly, 'he can't do that, can he?'

'I don't understand.'

'Your husband did. That's why he came. He wanted to know how I felt when I heard Billy Hopkins had died in jail.'

'That was the man who killed Karen?'

'If you can call him a man. I don't. But at least he's dead. Too quick, it was, for my liking.'

'How?'

'He hanged himself, in his cell.'

'Wasn't he watched? As a child murderer he'd have been in a special unit.'

'He was. Penned up like a pig in a sty,' Mrs Porter said with relish. 'The other prisoners made his life hell for what he did to Karen. He couldn't stand it any more.'

'How did you feel when you heard?' Sue had to relive what Colin experienced in this room with half-drawn curtains and no more life.

'Me? I don't feel anything any more, but my Karen can sleep peacefully now. The doctor's even been cutting back on my pills since the reporters come and told me.'

'You heard it from them first?'

39

'Yes. A whole crowd of them there was at the door. I shut it behind me and started to cry. For the first time since Karen was taken from me I could cry easy. I was still crying when the policewoman come back. Jane. She spent days with me when it happened. Come with me to court as well, she did. A nice girl, Jane. She cried too, that day we knew about Hopkins.'

'And that was what Colin wanted to know? How you felt about Hopkins?'

'Yes. He asked if I'd wanted him dead.' She looked pityingly at Sue. 'I ask you. What else? But I wanted to be the one.' Mrs Porter looked down at her hands. They were tense, claw-like. 'I wanted it to be slow, so's he'd suffer. I suppose if every day had become hell on earth until he topped himself, that's the best I could hope for.'

'Did you tell anyone that was what you wanted?'

'Anyone?' Mrs Porter snorted her amusement. 'I told the whole world I couldn't rest, nor could Karen, until that bastard was dead too.'

Sue had watched the quiet woman grieve and was astounded by the fury of anger, revenge, shaking the slight body opposite.

'Your husband,' Mrs Porter said at last. 'He wanted me to name names – the people I told. It was no good, there were just so many. I told him, anyone who come to the door.'

'Can you rest now?' Sue asked gently.

'Some nights I get to sleep quite well. I can even dream, with Karen running through a garden. It's not like the nightmares I used to get before that bastard topped himself.'

Sue left Burwell Close silent, withdrawn, her mind racing. What names was Colin searching for? What was the connection with his death? She was sure there must be one.

Sighing, Sue decided she must check in to the office and dialled, hoping there was no urgent need of her services.

'Sue! Where have you been? The Boss has been going spare! The *Globe*'s got a front page splash tomorrow and he wants you to do a special.' Sally was frantic. 'I've been trying to ring you for the last hour. Where the hell are you?'

Chapter Three

Sue hurried into the vast space of the *Journal* city room.

'Where the hell've you been?' Meg, the features editor, demanded to know. 'The old man's been going round the twist – and you know what he's like when he does that. We all suffer.'

Sue sped.

'And why, Miz Bennett, do you think I provide my staff writers with mobile phones? To keep up their image as yuppies? Why didn't you answer it?'

Jepson's bald dome shone with sweat and anger. His collar was strained, dangerously tight on a man with that kind of blood pressure.

'I've been at the London Hospital,' Sue said quietly, 'checking out some new data.'

'Meanwhile, back in the real world, the *Globe* looks like scooping us – thanks to you being unavailable.'

'Something drastic?'

'Not really.' The sarcasm seemed to relieve Jepson's bad humour a fraction. 'Headlines like "Pollution ends sex", and "Is macho-man endangered species?" Our readers are going to want to know what's up.'

Sue sighed. 'Oh, dear. They've translated animal research data to humans. The *Globe*'s decided we're all fish – or alligators.'

Heavy brows were drawn in a huge V, pointing along a thick, fleshy nose, down to the uncompromising line of a mouth. 'Give,' Jepson demanded, then lay back, swivelling in his massive leather chair.

'Fish are part of our food chain. Over the years they've picked up nonyl phenols which can be stored in fat. These phenols imitate female hormones, so developing male fish, bombarded by what passes for female instructions, stop developing testes and gee-up the ovary activity.'

Jepson pursed his lips. 'Go on.'

'Studies have been done on various species which seem to be having trouble producing healthy young males, and the evidence seems to agree. Nonyl phenols. When we eat fish, we get them as well.'

'You mean they can make human males sterile too?'

Sue considered her answer carefully. 'Yes. It's not only probable, it is likely men have been affected to some extent.'

'These – whatsit phenols. Explain.'

'Although some are used in paints and detergents, most are used in the plastics industry. This type of phenol helps make the material flow better in production. Harmful effects were first noticed in the States because of increased growth in cancer cells under research conditions. The doctors went spare trying to find the cause, then discovered it was in the plastic of the tubes they used. The industrialists wouldn't co-operate, so the medics did their own investigating. Nonyl phenols. It matched up with what other groups were doing and explained why male sea fish, and the alligators, were decreasing rapidly. About one third of all nonyl phenols in circulation end up in water. Sea water. Drinking water.'

'And that's how we come in contact?'

'The dilution would be too great to have any impact, no, it's probably through the food chain humans are at risk. The phenols presumably can't be broken down by the animals and are being stored and accumulated in fat. That's when it gets into us.'

'My God! What's been done about it?'

'Nonyl phenols are to be phased out by the year 2000.'

'And in the meantime?'

Sue grinned. 'Don't eat alligators.'

'It's no laughing matter,' she was rebuked with a growl. 'Just because it doesn't affect you women.'

'Probably not true, Mr Jepson. It won't turn us into men, but it does cause increased growth. Anything growing that shouldn't – well, we're on a hiding to nothing. It doesn't do anyone any good to be bathed in a sea of oestrogens.'

'I thought you said the trouble was –'

'Nonyl phenols can imitate oestrogens in animals.'

Jepson leaned forward. He picked up a pencil and kept stabbing it into his blotter. 'Right,' he decided. 'You – an article setting out the commonsense side of things.'

'Reassure readers they're safe? Best not to be too rosy in outlook. After all, there is supposed to be a general drop in human male sperm count. Phenols already in the system may partly account for that.'

'For Christ's sake, woman, are you trying to convince me I should say goodbye to my sex life? You'll be telling me next that male libido is a thing of the past – for young men, anyway,' he added smugly.

Sue looked at the paunch keeping him many inches away from his desk, at the hair which covered the backs of his hands and probably most of his body. She suppressed a shiver. If nonyl phenols could put him off women, they should be on prescription.

'A campaign,' Jepson barked. 'That's it. You set it up. Young Chalmers can be in charge of details. It's time he had a go at something – but I want you doing the explaining. Our readers need you.'

'But the phenols are being phased out anyway,' Sue protested.

'You know this country, and this bloody government. They all need a good boot up the backside if anything's to happen.'

Sue tried to look innocent. 'Perhaps a change of government would hurry things along,' she said sweetly.

True to form, Jepson's colour rose until the puce factor in his nose threatened disaster. 'Get going!' he barked.

Bobby Chalmers was delighted. He was small and bubbly with a mop of golden curls and blue eyes that hid a sharp mind. 'Great!' he exclaimed, when Sue told him what was expected. 'I'll go and natter with Paul. He'll know which MPs will be most sensitive on the subject. We can use them to harry the Min of Ag and Fish, or whatever it's called these days. This is going to be fun!'

It was hardly Sue's recipe for entertainment. Jepson's sudden obsession with the campaign was puzzling. To throw the whole weight of the *Journal* against a possible threat to the nation's virility seemed like a re-run of Don Quixote at his windmills. There were so many other causes which needed backing, worthwhile ones tackling starvation, crime, corruption. Why nonyl phenols, she wondered? Still, it was Jepson's paper, as he repeatedly told everyone, and his money.

By nine o'clock Sue was exhausted. With Bobby's help the battle plans were ready and all that remained was for Sue to visit researchers and find the up-to-date state of play. There would be a fair amount of travelling in the next day or so. She headed for Islington and her bed, feeling more like sleep than at any time in the last three weeks.

Letting herself into the flat Sue switched on the lights, grateful for the warmth, the peace. There might be no crushed raspberry dralon to be seen, but the flat had the stillness of the house in Burwell Close. There was the same absence of life.

Sue had stopped expecting to see Colin. It was only when she was unprepared and turned her head without thinking that she had the hope, the realization, the desolation. It was a sequence of emotions which had become depressingly familiar. The answerphone was blinking, so Sue ran it back and listened as she shed her coat and stretched her muscles the full length of the couch.

45

One caller had left no message. She kicked off her shoes and wiggled her toes. Her father's voice was in the room. 'Poppet – I hate these damned machines. Just had to let you know we're thinking of you. Mrs Stroat came back today. She was as near to apologizing as I've ever seen her. Very hopeful she hadn't offended you. Mum saw her off. Come and see us when you've time.'

The machine whirred. Two more blanks. Sue closed her eyes, sleep beginning to draw a veil over her mind. 'Sue?' It was Ken Miller. 'Sorry to bother you. I'm still short of a few papers for the files. If you do come across them lining a drawer, or stuffed behind a bookcase, I'd be glad of them. It is possible they were in the folder of Colin's personal things. No hurry. Leave it till the weekend.'

She was too tired to face any more sorting tonight. Sue would take his word the weekend would do.

'Pippa here.' The voice was a welcome sound. 'I've left the coffee and the Baileys with you. Have some before bed. You could have straight scotch, but it's not a good idea. My way's more fun. See you tomorrow. 'Bye.'

Sue looked at the clock. There was no need to ring Ken, he was not expecting her to call. It was much too late for her parents, they would worry if she phoned them at this hour, assuming she was having a panic attack. Picking up the phone, Sue dialled Pippa's number.

'Lo.' It was a sleepy voice which answered.

'I just rang to say thanks.'

'What for?'

'Just – thanks.'

'Tell me tomorrow.'

'That's why I've phoned now. I'll be off before you're awake, and away all day. Jepson's starting a campaign – at least, I'm doing it for him. I'm due at Brunel University at nine, then Reading Uni for lunch. I'll try and swing by my parents before coming home. I could be very late back.'

'Give them my love.'

46

'I will,' she promised.
''Night – sleep well.'

The meetings with the scientists were brief, to the point. It was a relief to talk in the jargon of the labs again, smell the indefinable mix which meant shining glassware, rubber bungs, cleaning fluids, a hint of xylene. Sue was happy to be back in an atmosphere which demanded her full concentration. Brunel might be one of the newer universities, but it had absorbed the aura and the aromas of its elders. Most of the staff she met were young, keen, anxious to discuss, while more senior figures showed caution, wary of a reporter in their midst. Even so, Sue filled gaps in her knowledge and was grateful for the courtesies.

The motorway station on the M4 was busy. Lunch was hot soup which congealed as she carried her tray to a table, and a sandwich which made chewing an aerobic exercise. In spite of giving herself ample time for the journey, Reading was congested, and Sue found it a challenge to reach her destination when she was expected. The professor's secretary produced excellent coffee. She also made sure Sue knew the great man's time was strictly rationed.

After leaving the book-lined office in Reading, Sue headed for her parents' house in Surrey, using quieter roads, the ones superseded by the M4 and the M25. It had been a good day, she thought. The gamut of emotions which stormed through her had been put on one side for a brief spell. Talking over facts with other scientists, drawing on memories, references, the academic side of her had surfaced, giving a breathing space. The wound she carried inside her was still as raw, but the sealing-off process had begun, the edges of her trauma puckering and pulling as they drew together.

The winter light was just beginning to fail as she went along the foot of Leith Hill and bypassed the centre of Dorking. Her parents were welcoming arms, familiar odours, reminding Sue she should get another bottle of her mother's perfume, ready for Christmas. They were so pleased to see her, disappointed it was a brief interlude. More food was thrust into the car, and three house plants her father had been nursing for her went in the boot, carefully wedged upright with the car blanket.

'I wish you could stay longer,' her mother said, love in her eyes.

'Next time, perhaps,' her father added, taking his wife's arm in consolation.

'I've got to make a call in Lewisham. It's a bit out of the way. Work's hotting up at the moment, so I can only go there tonight.'

'Drive carefully,' was caught by the wind as she went out on to the main road.

Rush-hour traffic kept Sue's mind from dwelling on all but the unfamiliar route to Lewisham. Her destination was a tower block, not far from Hither Green Hospital. Only when she had completed her errand and was driving home along London streets in the quiet period between work and play, did Sue have time to think.

The man who had answered her knock on the door in Lewisham wore the hopeless look of the long-term unemployed. Scrawny, he had stood in the doorway, his wife behind him. She was a large woman, covered in shapeless clothes, pale from too much washing. Her battle against the odds was marked in her face, her eyes. Mention of Colin's name had made the woman, Mrs Cahill, cry. A grubby tissue was dragged from between huge breasts and she used it to wipe away her tears, before spreading it as a shield from further hurt.

Mr Cahill had demanded to know why Colin had not been man enough to come back himself. When they knew the truth, Sue was hustled into the untidy living room. A pile of clothes was chucked over the back of the couch and she was urged to sit. Strong tea appeared, the hot liquid raw with Irish whiskey. For a moment it had been hard work for Sue not to giggle. Everyone seemed intent on pouring medicinal alcohol into her. At least it should help

48

thin her blood and prevent a heart attack, Sue reflected as she had sipped, but at what expense to her liver?

The photograph on the sideboard of the little room made Sue dread what she guessed she would hear. It was a formal portrait of a happy smiling girl, proud in the white dress of her first confirmation. Candles in glass holders flanked the frame. In front of it lay a rosary, and on the wall above, a crucifix. The parents took it in turn to tell Sue what was engraved in their memories.

Judy had been twelve. Missing only an hour or two, her ravished body had been discovered behind the pavilion in Mountsfield Park, right opposite the hospital complex where she had been born, and where her father had identified what was left of her.

Sue could hear Mr Cahill's voice still roaring in her head as she threaded through Camberwell's streets, heading for Southwark and Tower Bridge.

'The Old Bill knew who'd done it, straight off. They 'ad 'im inside double quick. That DNA proved it, not that they needed it. The bastard didn't even deny it. Just asked for 'is social worker.'

As the mother wept, the father had prowled round the room. 'Me and me missis went to court, to see him get sent down. Do you know what 'e did? The bugger smiled at me. 'E smiled!'

'It took 'alf the Bill to 'old him back, it did,' Mrs Cahill had said, pride in her husband breaking through sorrow.

'I wanted to do for 'im there and then,' little Judy's father had insisted.

Traffic lights stopped Sue, and she looked up at the majesty of Tower Bridge, a world away from the family rent apart by a cruel and senseless death.

'Where is he now?' Sue had wanted to know of Walker, the killer. 'Which jail?'

The parents had looked at each other, straightening a little with increased dignity.

'None,' Mr Cahill had told Sue.

'He's out already?'

'You might say.' Mrs Cahill had gone to the sideboard, picking up the photograph, tracing the frozen smile with her finger.

''Eart attack. Couldn't 'appen to a nicer bloke, but it was too quick. 'E should 'ave suffered.' Mr Cahill had tears in his voice as he looked down at his hands, clenched with anger.

Colin had been very nice, they told her. It had not seemed as if he were asking questions, just chatting, wanting to know who they had talked to of their hatred for Walker.

'Well, I mean ter say, we was out of our minds. Anyone at the door, I told 'em all. If I couldn't do for Walker meself, 'e should swing.' Mr Cahill had been very sure of his feelings.

Why had Colin been checking up on old murders? Sue asked herself the question for the umpteenth time as she arrived at her front door and searched in her bag for her keys. Hopkins had hanged himself two years ago, and it was fifteen months since Walker's fatal heart attack. Had they been clients of Colin's? She must ask Ken next time she saw him, Sue decided as she opened the door and went into the hall.

Instinct made her motionless, steady breathing reduced to the gentle flaring of nostrils as air passed in and was savoured. It was there, as Pippa had described. Aftershave. Not cheap exactly, but not a really good one. Sue listened intently. There was no sound. Holding her breath she listened for the slightest creak, the hint of someone else's breathing. Nothing.

Switching on the lights, Sue went through each room. She picked up the phone, dialled, waited.

'Pippa. He's been back. I can smell it.'

By the time Pippa arrived in the hall, there was no trace of the cologne.

'I was standing just where I am now, when I noticed something. Then, I didn't realize what made me stop.' Pippa was frowning, her high cheekbones thrown into prominence by the lights.

'It's exactly where I stopped,' Sue agreed.

'I wonder . . .' Pippa mused. 'Do you think he had to stand there for a while as he saw to the alarm? He couldn't do it with the door open, in case someone saw him.'

'And when he did open the door, it would be for a fraction of a second – leaving the smell behind.'

'So. We know he's been. What for? Any ideas?'

'There's no obvious sign of anything gone. I'll go and have another look.'

'I'll put the kettle on. This could be a long night.'

'Why?'

'You'll have to tell Bill and Ben.'

'The police? They were no use last time.'

'You still have to report it,' Pippa insisted. 'Now, go and look. I'll make some coffee.'

'With caffeine this time,' Sue groaned. 'I'm going to need it.'

Pippa was just depressing the handle of the cafetière when she heard Sue exclaim. 'What is it?' she called.

'My computer disks!' Pippa left the coffee to its own devices and ran to Sue.

'All of them?'

'I think so. There's none left, as far as I can see. I always kept them together.' Sue looked smaller, drooping as she stood in front of the open cabinet which had held the data she used for her work.

'Come on, my girl. Keep checking. If you have a big enough list of stolen goods, Bill and Ben might take you seriously – at last.'

It was a Bill and Benjamina who rang the doorbell just after midnight. Different people they may have been, but the attitude was the same.

'This is a little tricky, Mrs Bennett.' The woman was the sergeant and took the lead. 'It's rare we come across such a skilful burglar on our patch.'

'Are you suggesting it didn't happen?' Sue was indignant.

'Not at all,' she was soothed, 'but you must admit it is odd. There's no sign of forced entry, not tonight, or on the last occasion.'

'I was still robbed,' Sue insisted.

'Yes, madam,' the constable agreed. 'Funny, though.'

'Glad you think so,' Sue retorted.

'No, I mean it's strange the thief didn't take anything really valuable – in money terms,' he added hastily, as he saw Sue straighten up in anger. 'Round here, once they're in, they grab whatever they can flog quickly. Your husband's wallet didn't have any value that way, and your disks wouldn't be much use, even to the ordinary journalist. Only a scientist would be able to read them.'

'And that was all that went?' The sergeant wanted to press on. People had been hurt elsewhere, she had her priorities.

'A folder of papers.'

'Yours?' Sue was asked.

'No. Personal papers belonging to my husband. I hadn't had time to go through them, so I don't know what they contained.'

'Right, Mrs Bennett.' The sergeant was brisk, standing as she put away her notebook.

'You didn't give a key to anyone, did you?' the constable asked. He was comfortable in the warm flat and the coffee had been good. He was in no hurry. 'I mean,' he went on, 'no sign of intrusion.'

'No, I did not.'

'It's not easy to say this, circumstances being what they are, but could your husband have done so? Given someone a key?' The implication of illicit sex hung in the air.

'You're suggesting Colin had a mistress here?' Pippa threw herself into battle as Sue sat rigid, appalled. 'There's no way that could have happened, neither emotionally, nor practically. Mrs Bennett's reported the thefts, it's your turn to get off your backside and do something.'

'Well, Mrs Bennett.' The sergeant thought it time she took back control of events. 'If you could come down to the station and make a statement, I would be very grateful. We'll do what we can.'

Sue kept her composure until the door closed behind them, then the tears began.

'Bed, for you,' Pippa said firmly. 'And I'm staying the night on the couch.'

'In case Colin's mistress comes back, wearing some God-awful aftershave?' The bitterness was tearing at her.

'Perhaps she has a big black moustache,' Pippa said calmly. 'Do you think she uses an electric razor?'

Sue giggled, a faint sound of returning sanity.

'Mind, you have to look at it from their point of view. Your data could have been taken in a fit of jealousy.'

'Colin's papers?'

'She might have thought he'd named her in them somewhere.'

'And left them where I could read it? She didn't know Colin.'

'Exactly. Because there was no other female – and you know it.'

Jepson was in his office waiting for her next morning. 'You're late!' he barked.

'I'm sorry. I did phone in. After the locksmith had been, I had to go and make a statement. Thefts from the flat.'

'Sorry,' he begrudged. 'Much damage?'

'None.'

Massive eyebrows winged away in surprise. 'You were lucky.'

Sue thought of the woman who had sat next to her in the police station waiting room. Elderly, respectable, she had cried. The thieves had taken her few bits of jewellery, that was bad enough, and the money she had saved for her holiday with her son and his wife. The worst part, she had told Sue, was the vandalism. The furniture made precious by years of use and care had been smashed beyond repair, the walls daubed with excrement. The smell was clean when compared with the state of mind of the perpetrators.

'Yes,' Sue agreed with her employer. 'I was lucky.'

'Now, this campaign.'

He was brought up to date with the progress Sue and Bobby Chalmers had made.

'We've reached the point where we need your decision,' Sue told him. 'One possibility is that we just do it in-house, using our own people and reaching our existing readers. The other way is to go national. It would mean bringing in a good ad agency – Maginty's perhaps. That way we could get radio and TV coverage. It would also mean using you, personally.' She smiled sweetly. The gun had been cocked and aimed. Would he pull the trigger?

'How?'

The imaginary finger was tensing on the curve of the metal.

'Posters which would include you and, perhaps, an appropriate government minister. How far the campaign goes would depend on how much you are prepared to underwrite Maginty. It should increase readership.'

'Mm. Sounds feasible. You scientists certainly believe in looking ahead. Leave it with me. I'll get on to Maginty's – and I've a friend in Downing Street who owes me a favour or two.'

Jepson was so predictable, Sue thought as she left the office. Study his ego and you could direct him the way you wanted him to go.

'Did he buy it?' Bobby Chalmers was just round the corner, waiting anxiously.

Sue smiled and circled a thumb and first finger. 'On the button.'

Bobby capered, his delight knocking him against a

stately secretary. Sue left him to his apologies. With Jepson and Bobby fielding the campaign to their mutual glory, she might get a little more peace.

Heading for her desk, Sue was halted by Clive Bauman, his plump body immaculate in the dark suit which ensured him courtesy in the law courts he haunted.

'No joy on that inquest transcript, Sue. Sorry. No copy available, apparently. Damned odd, that.' Lines scored the narrow forehead.

'Who would have it?'

Clive shrugged his shoulders. 'Colin's insurers?'

'But why would they need it now? The verdict was an accident.'

'Who knows? Strange cattle, insurers.'

'Clive.'

He looked intently at Sue.

'The transcript. It was a purely personal request.'

Clive smiled and drew a finger across his lips as though closing a zip.

Sue wore a puzzled expression as she sat at her desk and dialled a number. 'Mr Miller, please,' she told the girl on the answering switchboard. 'Ken? Sue Bennett. Sorry if I'm holding you up. I've had another theft. All my computer disks, and the folder you said I should look through at the weekend. Was there anything in it I needed? I ask because there's a possibility Colin's insurers have the transcript of the inquest. I asked for a sight of it, but there's no copy available. It's on the cards the insurance company have it.'

'Yes, it's possible.' There was a silence. 'Listen, Sue. We're both busy at the moment. Come out to dinner tonight. There are some good restaurants near you.'

'I'm not sure. I don't really want to go out. Why not let me cook for you – at least heat up one of my mother's offerings.'

'No, Sue – but thank you. It's important, or I wouldn't ask.'

Sue was mystified. 'If you say so, Ken. Of course.'

'I'll be outside your flat in the car at seven thirty.'

The Greek restaurant was busy, but there were quiet corners. Ken ushered Sue to a small table isolated from its neighbours.

'Thank you for coming.'

'I wasn't trying to be awkward,' Sue told him. 'It's just so soon after . . .'

'I understand – believe me, I do. I had my reasons for being so persistent.'

She looked at his face, dark and intent as he studied the menu. 'Something's worrying you. Is it to do with Colin?'

'I don't know. Perhaps. It certainly concerns you.'

'The burglaries?'

Ken nodded. 'The first one. I'm guessing it happened the first time your home had been left empty since Colin died.'

Sue thought back, trying to remember days, times, in the abyss. 'Yes, it was. Pippa was with me until my parents came. After that, Pippa or my mother stayed in because of the phone.'

'Who knew you'd be away all day yesterday?'

'Anyone at the *Journal* who was interested, although I doubt many would be. Bobby – Bobby Chalmers, he's my assistant. Then Sally, one of the secretaries who has to keep track of me. Beth – she usually sub-edits my copy. Matthew Jepson, perhaps. He's the editor and I'm working on a campaign he's anxious to shine in, but I'm very small fry for him to bother about.'

'What about your parents?'

'No, I don't think so. I only rang and told them I was on my way to see them when I was due to leave Reading.'

'Think, Sue,' Ken said urgently. 'Did you talk to anyone about your plans for yesterday, especially on the phone.'

'No. I left so early, I didn't ring anyone.'

56

Sue sat with her face propped on her hands, her eyes closed. She was so tired. Proper sleep had eluded her since Colin had died. Her mind began to wander off on its own course. With an effort she wrenched her concentration back to the present.

'The night before,' Ken urged. 'What time did you get in?'

'Late. It was after ten.' Sue was back in the quiet flat, switching on the answerphone and yielding to the inviting length of the couch. 'Three people called but left no message. There was one from my father, nothing important. Then there was yours.' Her eyes opened wide, and she stared at Ken. 'You talked about the folder, said there was no hurry.'

'Did you ring anyone?'

Sue was back in time, trying to follow the sequence of events. 'Pippa. I just wanted to thank her and say goodnight.'

'Was that all?' He sounded disappointed.

'No. Pippa said she'd see me tomorrow . . .' Sue's voice trailed into silence, shock appearing in her eyes, the lines of her face.

'And you told her you'd be out all day.'

'Yes, but you can't think Pippa –'

'Of course not, but can't you see the logic of the situation? I talk about the papers you have, how there are sheets I need. You tell Pippa you'll be away next day, and hey presto, you get a visit from the smelly burglar who whips away the file, and all your data – just in case.'

A smiling waiter brought a tray of appetizers, the colours of the salads tempting. He busied himself attending to their needs, not leaving until they began to eat with obvious enjoyment.

Ken speared and ate an olive.

Sue pushed sliced tomatoes around in their dressing of oil. 'So. The phone's bugged. But why? Why me?'

'I don't think it is you, so much as what you may have in the flat.'

'Had. I suppose I must be grateful the whole place didn't get trashed.'

'Yes, you are,' Ken agreed. 'If anyone wanted to make it look like a normal burglary, anything saleable would have gone, the rest – wrecked. Whoever's behind this doesn't want you upset too much.'

'You're joking!' She saw the grim line of his mouth, the seriousness of his expression. 'No, you're not, are you?'

'I think it's to do with Colin. It's not something he was working on for the firm – I've taken over his cases and nothing has happened with them to make me suspicious. It seems to be related to Colin's private life.'

'Don't you start trying to tell me his mistress is coming out of the woodwork!'

Ken laughed, an infectious sound in the dim corner of the aromatic little room. 'Who on earth thought that?'

'A moron laughingly known as a detective. He had that bright idea about two o'clock this morning.' Sue smiled grimly, remembering. 'Pippa tore strips off him.'

'Good for her.'

The waiter deftly removed plates, straightened cutlery, and fussed with the wine bottle before he left them in peace.

Ken leaned forward. 'Judith collected all Colin's personal things from his desk. She's stored them in Bill Farnum's office. I know people are in and out all day, many of them total strangers. We have a certain amount of security, but at night the cleaners are in, and I should imagine anyone wanting to go through Colin's possessions would find it easy enough.'

'But it, whatever it is, could be at home?'

He nodded. 'You've got to face facts, Sue. Your flat's been watched. Perhaps you have too. Your phone is probably bugged, and I doubt the Home Office agreed to it. I know you haven't had much joy with the police, but I'd like you to talk to a friend of mine. He's still in the force, and he's a good copper. Damned good.'

Sue was startled. 'You think it's that serious?'

'Yes. I do.'

Succulent lamb, falling away from whitened bones, appeared on plates before them. Vegetables were served, sauces provided, their opinions sought. At last, the waiter went away.

Sue played with her fork, twirling it to reflect the light. 'Will he help me find out who killed Colin?' She looked calmly at Ken. 'I believe he was deliberately pushed in front of that train.'

Ken was silent, looking down at his plate. He raised his head and looked intently at Sue. What she read in his expression made her sigh with relief.

'You do, too. Don't you?'

Chapter Four

Sue felt safe, comfortable, in the sparely furnished, functional rooms of Ken's Battersea flat. 'Is your friend coming?' she asked as they were settled into chairs, the electric fire turned up a bar.

'Stephen's off duty soon. He'll come straight here.'

'No wife to get back to?' from Pippa.

'No, a girlfriend. She's away.'

Ken handed them some menus. 'I hope you don't mind a take-away? The Cantonese restaurant round the corner's very good. I'm a very regular customer.'

The food had been delivered and steaming cartons were revealing their contents when the bell rang. Ken jumped up to answer it.

'Just in time,' he told his guest, introducing Stephen Childs to the two women.

The newcomer was tall, solid, brown-haired, and with a firm handshake. He stripped off coat, scarf, with economical movements, before mounding rice in his bowl. They ate Chinese fashion, lifting rice with chopsticks, picking morsels from the containers.

'This is marvellous,' Pippa decreed, nibbling with sharp white teeth at the tail of a king prawn.

'Every time I see Ken these days, I seem to eat,' Sue said, finding strips of marinaded beef to her liking.

'Not before time,' Pippa retorted. 'You were getting too thin.'

Sue lowered her eyes. 'I just didn't seem to feel hungry.'

Stephen Childs looked at her. 'Understandable. But

I gather you're a medical journalist.' He grinned, looking suddenly younger, more boyish. 'I expect you could tell us exactly how long the human female can go without food. As long as you had water –'

'Tea,' Sue said with feeling. 'Oceans of it.'

'That reminds me,' said Ken, rising to his feet. 'Wine? Lager?'

It was restful, the music Pippa had selected adding to the harmony. When no one could eat any more, Ken rose and began to clear away the debris.

'Let me help,' Pippa offered, gathering empty glasses. 'You stay put,' she told Sue firmly.

Tired, Sue lay back in her chair, Stephen Childs watching her.

'I'm sorry about your husband.'

As with Mrs Willoughby, the crisp words conveyed real meaning. 'Thank you.'

'Ken's filled me in. It seems the first thing to do is to get your flat swept.'

A shadow of a smile flickered. 'I assume you mean for bugs, not dust?' Sue asked.

Stephen answered her with a grin, green flashing in the hazel of his eyes. 'Although it could have been done straight away, I've arranged it for tomorrow. We have to make sure whoever has planted it doesn't get suspicious that you're on to them.'

'Is that so important?'

'Yes. We can learn more about them, that way.' Reaching into an inside pocket, he took out a small card and, leaning across the coffee table, handed it to Sue. 'Ring that number first thing and tell them your cleaner's playing up – you can't get it to suck properly, that sort of thing. Malcolm will arrange a time. A great guy, Malcolm – and an electronics whizz kid. When he does come, do exactly what he tells you. You may find it means written instructions.'

'It sounds very cloak and dagger.'

'That's who he normally works for – but he owes me a favour.'

Sue drooped a little. She was tired, and to know that others believed her and were prepared to help, brought tears dangerously near the surface.

'Your disks.'

She looked up. 'They've been stolen.'

'And the back-up ones too?'

Her eyes widened. 'How did you guess?'

'Ken told me. You were furious you'd been robbed, but you'd not gone berserk – which would have happened if all your work data had gone for a burton.'

'After Colin died, I kept myself busy at the computer – all the jobs I'd been meaning to do. Tidying up files, sorting and copying disks. That way I didn't have to think.'

'Makes sense. So, where are they?'

She hesitated.

'You have to trust somebody.' He nodded towards the kitchen from whence came the chink of crockery, chat, the occasional laugh. 'Those two, for a start. Ken was a damned fine detective. I'd trust him with my life. How about Pippa?'

'Yes, I can trust Pippa.'

'But you don't want the chance of a word going astray, being heard by the wrong ears?'

Sue nodded. 'I just have the feeling it's close to home. Am I being silly?'

'No.'

'Coffee, you two?' It was Pippa, head round the door, who asked.

Stephen looked at Sue, who nodded. 'Please,' he said, and Pippa disappeared.

Sue was irresolute, drumming with her fingers on the arm of the chair.

'Something else is worrying you. Can I help? It's why I came.'

She told him about the list she had found in Colin's wallet. It was safe at home now, tucked away where no burglar would dream of looking. She leaned down and from her handbag took a printed copy.

'This was amongst his belongings returned by the police. It was the only thing not stolen, the first time round.'

Stephen read quickly, looking up in surprise. 'These names are all too familiar. They would be to any policeman.' There was a question in his tone.

'I visited the first two,' Sue explained, adding a very brief account of her conversations with Mrs Porter, the Cahills, the questions Colin had asked them. 'I don't know if I could get to all of them. I'm assuming they are families of murder victims?'

'Yes.' He tapped the list. 'The Stockton boy – that was a few years back. Some of these took a while to solve, but the men responsible were all caught eventually and convicted.'

'Would you be able to find out dates for me? I'm sure there's information locked up in our morgue.'

'Of course. I'll give Ken a nod. He can get a message to you without it looking obvious.'

'Thank you. Oh, is it possible for you to trace the men in jail? Where they are now? I know about the first two on the list. They're dead.'

As Stephen nodded, puzzled, Pippa led the way in with a dish of chocolate biscuits, Ken following with a tray of coffee.

'Sue, the transcript. Did you mention it?' Pippa asked.

'What transcript?' Ken asked.

'The inquest,' Sue explained, accepting a mug from Pippa and clasping the warmth with both hands. 'Our legal department couldn't get a copy.'

'That's odd,' Stephen said. 'Press people can usually lay hands on them easier than we can. Why do you want it?'

'I don't. Not all of it. It's just one of the witnesses. I saw his expression.' Sue told of her instincts that he had been troubled when asked to interpret the movement on the platform.

'A copy of the security video would be more help. Any chance?' Ken asked Stephen.

'Could be. It's worth a try.'

'This crusade Jepson's wittering on about. Anything in it for me?' Watson Skinner leaned on Sue's terminal.

'You, Watty?'

'Possible explanation of crimes of violence soaring amongst pubescent males? Perhaps they sense they're losers in the mating stakes and have to lash out at those more successful?'

'If you can find a link between tearaways and trout, good luck,' Sue laughed. 'There's an element of truth, I suppose, but it has a very tenuous link to crime figures.'

'Enough for an article?'

'I know how you work. You could turn it into a series, and have MPs being lobbied.'

'You rate me too highly, Sue,' Watty told her. 'Still, it's a thought. More boys than girls these days, thanks to you blasted scientists. Bright girls getting the best jobs – like some people I could mention.' His grin took any sting from his words. 'For the average spotty, adolescent youth, a dose of female hormone in his cod and chips might be just enough to make the poor devil wonder who he is, and take it out on the next person who comes along looking happy.'

'Are you excusing them? The yobs?' Sue asked quietly.

'No way!' Watty's frown was dark, brooding. 'There are no extenuating circumstances for any of the little bastards!'

The words were vehement, shocking Sue. Watty recovered his equanimity quickly, and smiled.

'I just want to point out to our dear readers the more of this scum that floats to the surface, the harder we have to work to skim it off and burn it.'

'Flame throwers instead of the gallows? A change of direction for you, Watty.'

'When you clean up the rubbish in the garden, you eradicate pests in it with fire. It's the best way to keep the plants healthy.'

'I know you can keep this argument going indefinitely, and with every possible metaphor, but I have to get home.'

'You're leaving wee Chalmers in charge?'

Sue smiled. 'Hardly in charge. He's just doing all the running round for our Great White Chief.'

'Watch him, Sue,' Watty advised. 'He's after your job.'

'Bobby?' She shook her head. 'No. It's Jepson who needs to watch out. It's his shoes Bobby wants to fill.'

Watty threw back his head. 'Agh! Thank God! If it was his pants he was after now, he'd have to take half-a-dozen of his little buddies in with him. The thought intrigues!'

Sue laughed, an infectious sound. 'Watty, you're dreadful – but good for me.'

He was suddenly serious. 'How goes it, Sue? Are you coping?'

'Yes.' The answer was a little hesitant, then, 'Yes, I am, thank you.' She stood and began to pick up her bag and briefcase, checking the pocket of her jacket for her keys. 'I must get home. The vacuum's on the blink and the repairman said he'd be there at midday.'

'Call me if you need anything. Anything at all.'

'I will,' she promised, and hurried away.

Sue had been at home only five minutes when the doorbell rang. The man wearing faded blue workman's overalls was very tall, loose-limbed.

'Mrs Bennett? I'm Malcolm Goss. Your vac's playing up, they told me in the office.'

The accent had the broadness of south London, not the easy vowels of the Caribbean Sue expected after she had looked up at the great height of the man at the door. 'Come in.'

Whistling, Malcolm Goss put down the holdall he had

been carrying, and from it drew equipment, assembling it quickly. 'Let's have a look at this machine of yours,' he said, aiming the working end of his gadget at the pictures in the hall.

Sue went to the kitchen and obediently trundled the cleaner from its hiding place, giving Malcolm the chance to check further.

'Before I start, can I use your loo?' he asked.

'Of course,' Sue agreed, guessing the bathroom would be electronically swept in the process.

He reappeared, but from the bedroom, shaking his head and smiling cheerfully 'OK, mam. To work.'

While Sue watched, he dismantled the outer casing of the cleaner then gave her a running account of his actions. It fascinated her to see an expert at work. Anyone listening in would be convinced it was a routine maintenance, but Sue saw her sitting room checked, grid-fashion.

'No, mam, nothing serious at first sight.' Goss aimed the detector at the phone and nodded his head as the dials jumped. 'I think I can see what's wrong.' He pointed to the phone, and then to his lips, emphasizing care. 'Did you, at some time, have a thread, a piece of string caught up when you were vacuuming?'

'Yes. I think so,' she answered to his encouraging nod.

'That's it, then. It's caused a partial burn-out in this little gismo here. Don't worry, I carry a spare. Soon have you functioning on all cylinders.'

A screwdriver in his left hand was used to keep up sounds of repair while Malcolm wrote quickly on a pad.

Sue read the note and nodded understanding. She would follow instructions. 'I was just about to have a sandwich and coffee. Would you like some?' she invited.

'Great. A frame like mine, you never say no to free food.' The grin was real, warm and unscripted. 'Can I use your phone? The battery of my mobile's died on me and the boss will want to know when I'm free for the next job.'

She watched him as she waited for the kettle to boil. With incredible speed the phone was opened and he showed her a tiny piece of engineering that looked too innocent to harm her. With the phone back in action, he dialled and waited.

'Twenty minutes, Guv. That OK? Mrs Bennett's just making me a bite of lunch while I finish, then I'll be on my way. Only one fault as far as I can see. It's been no hassle.'

Crockery clinked in the kitchen, water swished from the tap. Malcolm hummed a tune with a catchy beat as he dried his hands. His long, narrow face was intent as he wrote another note. '1 unit only, voice-activated, i.e. by phone, answerphone, conversation in flat.'

Sue was silent, wondering if the intruder had been able to monitor her crying, her bouts of pain that knew no ease. 'Have a sandwich,' she said, then scribbled, 'What do I do?'

'Thanks. These look good.' The answer took longer. 'Today nothing. Just remember it's there. Tonight, tomorrow, drop the phone so you damage it. Better get mad and throw it.'

She read, then looked at him, puzzled. 'Damage?' she wrote.

'That's the idea. Chuck it out and get a new phone,' she read.

'Complicated?'

'No. Bug is very pricey. Someone may try to get it out of your bin. It will tell us more if they do.'

After showing her the notebook, Malcolm clattered his empty mug on to his plate and straightened up. 'Well, thanks for that. Very welcome indeed, Mrs Bennett. You shouldn't have any more trouble with your machine now – as long as you remember what made it go wrong this time.' He smiled at her, reassurance in his eyes, then scrawled swiftly, 'Have you changed your locks?'

'Locksmith here yesterday,' she wrote and he nodded approval. 'You want me to sign here?' she asked.

'Please, if you're satisfied?'

'Very, and thank you.'

*   *   *

Contact with the office was all too easy by computer, and Sue was kept busy. Fifty words on acupuncture to be added to an interview with an ageing TV star. Two hundred on CFCs. A memo from Sam Haddleston, the deputy editor, took longer. He wanted the main points on abuse of anabolic steroids.

Pippa came and went with undemanding company and hot drinks, making Sue relax. Tiredness was a thing of muscle and bone, of eyelids aching, but too hot to close.

Mrs Lavin called her, the love in the voice undoing Sue's self-control. When her mother finished speaking, Sue held the phone at arm's length. 'Why, Colin? Why can't it ever be you I hear again on this damned thing.'

There was no need for acting, her fury was real, helplessness assuaged in the violence with which she threw the instrument from her and on to the tiles of the hearth. Plastic splintered, and with it her attempts to be calm. Weeping, she lay on her bed, once again feeling the rawness of the open wound as it screamed for relief.

Next morning Sue was grim, determined, hiding the night's ravages with make-up. From the hearth she picked up the pieces of the useless phone, carrying it like dead vermin to the waste bin in the kitchen. She thought of what would happen when, like a good citizen, she emptied her little pieces of refuse into the larger mass to be hauled away A bubble of energy began to invade her muscles. Opening a cupboard, Sue found a packet of ready-made custard. Scissors opened up a wide gap and Sue poured a steady yellow stream, thick and all-pervading, over the wreckage of her phone, making sure the innocent-looking little bug was well and truly soaked.

If anyone wanted the bug back, they were well and truly welcome to it.

The *Journal* office had its usual sound level, computer keys almost silenced by the hum of machines, the buzz of voices.

'Sue! Darling! Haven't had a chance to chat, you've been on the move!' It was Kate, overdressed and overbearing, who perched on Sue's desk. 'The old man's being self-important at a CBI meeting, and that foul little cherub you usually have trailing you is behaving as though he was God's gift. Certainly not to women, if all I've heard about him is true.'

'Bobby? What's he done now?'

'Don't ask,' Kate groaned. 'Clive and I are conspiring to get the little queen. It's best you don't know. You're so honest, Sue, it shows in your face, and you just might give the game away.' Kate was immobile, her perfume warring with tobacco fumes as she watched Sue at work. 'I wish I could help,' she said wistfully.

Sue looked up, startled, surprised to see real concern in Kate's eyes.

Kate lit another cigarette with a flourish, masking the glimpse of her emotions with a wry twitch of her lips. 'Been there, done that, got the T shirt, as they say. It's a do-it-yourself hell. Mind, I was younger than you. Nineteen and pregnant. He had cancer and I lost the baby. I muddled through, I suppose. Never risked it again, though.'

'I didn't know you'd been married. I'm sorry.'

The cigarette waved nonchalantly. 'It was a long time ago. Mostly I make sure I never remember. What happened to you brought it all back.'

For a moment there was a pool of stillness around the desk. 'You're right,' Sue said at last.

'Of course, but specifically?'

'A do-it-yourself hell.'

Kate drifted away and Sue looked at her list of work due. She was checking data on leukaemia clusters and power cables when Sandy Jackson disturbed her.

'I need inspiration, Sue. These damned Germans look as though they're going to get British beef banned after all. It'll be against the EC laws, and that's something they don't like us playing at. Have you got anything I can use? Anything at all? Something we could ban from Germany?'

Memories began clicking like safe tumblers in Sue's memory. 'If I remember rightly . . .'

'And you usually do.'

She looked at him, startled. Sandy was serious. 'Foot and mouth,' she said.

'I didn't think we had it.'

'Exactly. But it's rife in Poland and it will be back here if we go on getting Polish cattle brought in via Germany.'

'Good girl! I knew I could rely on you!'

'That's OK. I like to know my steak's safe too, you know.'

Assignments completed, Sue packed up and was ready to go home.

'Glad I caught you.' It was Bobby Chalmers. He had taken to wearing braces, like Jepson. On Bobby's small frame with its tiny waist, they looked ridiculous, a little boy aping the grown-ups. 'I need an update on new material.'

'You need it?' she asked quietly.

He flushed a little. 'Jepson wants it. I said I'd ask you.'

'That's different. I'll give Faye a memo for him.'

'I can deal with it.'

'You've got to learn about Jepson. He may send me a message through you, but he expects a report from me personally,' she chided gently.

Bobby smiled sweetly, but Sue had a feeling he had hoped to lure her into taking a wrong step with Jepson. Mrs Stroat was right, she thought. Young men queuing up because she was vulnerable. The one in front of her was ready to exploit any moment of weakness she might have, but not to invade her bed and her bank balance.

The memo to Jepson was soon completed, Sue informing him of a visit to a professor friend who would have all the latest gossip on the research into nonyl phenols. To guarantee Bobby could not undermine her in any way, Sue did not add that the professor was in Edinburgh.

The air shuttle north next morning was bumpy, turbulence making the stewardess lurch as she poured coffee for Sue. It diverted both of them from the sounds of a passenger nearby using the bag tucked away for just such an occasion. The pilot made a very creditable landing in spite of the driving wind and rain, and it was not long before Sue was in a taxi heading for the university.

The professor she had met before. He welcomed Sue with a smile and an offer of lunch, pleased when she suggested the *Journal* feed him wherever he chose.

'A bribe, Sue?'

'Recompense, perhaps,' she laughed.

He drove to a large, secluded hotel on the city's outskirts. The food, as he had promised, was marvellous, even Sue enjoying the meal.

'I can drive you to the airport,' the professor offered, when the last of the coffee had been drunk. 'What time's your plane?'

'That's very kind of you, but I have to go to Glasgow first. I'd be grateful of a lift to the station,' Sue said with a smile.

The train west was swift and at Glasgow Central she soon found a taxi. In Maryhill, the driver stopped outside a tenement block. Sue had noticed battered phone boxes, a scarcity of taxis.

'Can you come back for me?' she asked the driver.

He seemed unsure, shaking his head dubiously.

'I'll make it worth your while,' she promised. 'An hour. If I'm not waiting here, I'll be in that cafe over there.'

He left and Sue went up the stairs, a mixture of smells assailing her nose. There was bleach, decay, curry, urine. Some of the doors looked as though careful people lived inside, while others were daubed with graffiti. It was on one such door she knocked.

'Mrs McGovern?' Sue asked the woman who answered.

'Who wants to knaw?'

71

'My name is Bennett. My husband died very recently. Amongst his things was a list of names and addresses. Yours was one.'

'Reporter, was he?' The woman sighed, hitching up the baby sprawled across her hip.

'No. He was a solicitor.'

'We've nae call for lawyers. Seen enough o' them to last a lifetime.'

'I understand. Because of your little girl?'

Suspicion appeared, tightening lax muscles. 'What d'you want?'

'Just to talk to you. I think my husband planned to do so – but he was killed before he could come.'

'When?'

'A month ago.'

The woman's face crumpled. 'Come ben,' she said.

Sue was not clear what was expected of her until Mrs McGovern opened the door wider and gestured Sue into the flat. The tiny rooms were clean, tidy, drab, except for the space in front of the coal fire where there was a playpen. The baby, a boy, was deposited inside the pen and Sue invited to sit. Haltingly at first, Sue explained the reason for her being there.

'I know my husband would have asked you what you thought of the sentencing.'

A snort of disgust startled the baby who turned to look at his mother. 'They should nae ha bothered wi' the little runt. Best the vetinry put him down.'

As the mother went on talking Sue had a feeling of *déjà vu*. A murdered child, distraught parents. The McGoverns had stayed together, drawn closer by grief.

'It was wee Patrick who could nae manage. Wet beds, greetin'. Bernadette was his twin, ye ken.'

To be nine years old and have the other half of you torn away with such brutality. Sue's tears added to the mother's.

'How is he now?' Sue wanted to know.

'Better. When we heard yon de'il was deid, we a' could breathe again.'

'He's dead?' Sue had expected it, but she had to make sure. 'How?'

'A sharpent spoon. Easy in Barlinnie for them as ken the ropes. Aye, Campbell, the bastard, he'd kilt afore, but he'll no kill again.'

'Bernadette was not the first?'

'Three ithers. A' wee girls. Mebbe they had uncles in Barlinnie.' Mrs McGovern crossed herself. 'They hae ma thanks.'

The wind had dropped a little by the time the plane left Glasgow Airport. Take-off was fairly smooth and the turbulence less dramatic than on the morning flight. Sue had time to make notes of her meeting with the professor, listing the odd snippets of information he had passed on. That done, she settled back in her seat and shut her eyes, but images flickered to and fro behind the closed lids. Mrs McGovern was there, the baby, growing up in a family already wrecked by callous lust. What kind of life could it have? It would be well loved and fiercely protected. Maybe that would be enough.

The engines droned on towards Heathrow. The Cahills would have got through another day, she thought, Mrs Porter, too. The shrine which had been a child's bedroom would have been cleaned yet again, fresh flowers scenting the still air. In another part of London was Mr Porter holding his new baby, not letting its mother know just how hard he was praying this scrap of warm humanity was not slain.

What was it Colin had been after, Sue puzzled? She drowsed in the warm air of the cabin, her thoughts and images racing, tumbling at the edge of her consciousness. Perhaps she did sleep. Colin was there, smiling, nodding approval, then she was wakened by a ringing sound. Seat belts were to be fastened and, heavy-eyed, Sue watched the lights of a wintry London appear.

It was not long before Sue was in her car and shivering as she headed home from Heathrow. It was late enough for the traffic to be easy and she was soon fitting her keys in the door, grateful for the rush of warm air which surrounded her in the hall. She sniffed. There was no smell of aftershave.

Next morning, Sue was heading for the bathroom when she saw that a note had been slipped under her front door. It was from Pippa.

'Got home too late to wake you,' Sue read. 'Have some information for you from Stephen. Come up before you go to Wapping.'

Sue did as she had been bid, her knock answered by a sleepy Pippa, tousled hair soft in the early light.

'Come in,' she urged Sue. 'Don't mind the mess. I went out in a hurry last night and just left things as they were.'

Painting materials were spread on the huge drawing board where Pippa worked. In spite of her haste, Sue noticed the brushes had been cleaned. She smiled to herself. Artists and scientists were not so different after all. Method was important to them both.

'The envelope's on the drawing board,' Pippa called from the kitchen.

'Thanks.' Sue opened it and went swiftly through the lists Stephen had prepared for her. Stomach muscles tightened involuntarily as her tentative theory was confirmed. 'How did you come by this?' she asked as she leaned against the kitchen door, watching Pippa pour water into coffee mugs and extract toast from the machine.

'Ken phoned me, because the paper told him you were away for the day. We met last night.'

Was it the heat of the toaster, or was Pippa blushing, Sue wondered?

'Pleasant?'

'Yes, it was. Very.' Pippa was a little defensive. 'Do you mind?'

'You seeing Ken? Heavens, no. I think it's a great idea.'

'But he's your friend,' Pippa argued.

'Yes. A friend. That's all,' Sue said firmly.

Bobby Chalmers was waiting for her when Sue arrived at her desk.

'Have you got the update?' he wanted to know.

'Yes, thank you,' she said, smiling at him. 'I'll report it verbally to Jepson.'

'I'm to see him at ten. I could take a memo from you.'

'That's kind, but I talked to him yesterday from Edinburgh. He wants me in his office at nine-thirty.'

The small pink mouth primmed in disapproval, while Sue tried hard not to grin.

'Perhaps we could go in together?' Bobby persisted.

'I think not. It's not wise to alter any appointments Jepson's made. He doesn't like it,' Sue warned. 'Now, has anything interesting come up overnight?'

Jepson was his usual curt self. 'Well?' he barked. 'Airfare to Scotland worth it?'

'Very much so. The professor is in touch with all the labs working on nonyl phenols. Over a good lunch he was prepared to gossip.'

'I suppose the food cost the earth?'

'Not as much as plane tickets to the States would have done if he hadn't told me all I wanted to know from that neck of the woods.'

Jepson nodded approval and almost smiled at Sue. Her acerbity was returning, she was coming back to life.

'Any more thoughts on this business?'

'Watty Skinner's the one you should talk to.'

'Why?' Jepson demanded.

Sue explained Watty's theory of the reasons for increased violence amongst inadequate young males.

'I suppose what we need is a bloody good war,' Jepson growled.

'Certainly not. The Flanders trench type would shift numbers back, but we don't get that kind of battle any more. The new ones wipe out too many women and children. It would just worsen the situation.'

'So, what do we do?'

'Leave it to nature.'

Sue left Jepson to his imagination and Bobby Chalmers. Imagination should keep Jepson awake at night, worrying about his libido and his sperm count. As for Bobby, having chosen his way of life he was hardly a frustrated loser in the mating game. Perhaps the two men deserved each other? No women did, Sue was sure about that.

She headed for the *Journal*'s morgue. It was clean, dust-free, well-lit. Banks of stored microfilm occupied one wall, screens for viewing another. Sue sighed, remembering such a place in Fleet Street when she had been part of a school visit. There had been a smell of knowledge, a sense of standing in history. Now? All she had was a feeling that all past facts and opinions were merely fodder for a demanding present.

Using the list Stephen Childs had sent her, Sue found the dated microfilm she needed, and worked quickly through the sheets. Occasionally she stopped to copy anything relevant, and by the time she had finished, there was a sizeable pile of print. Most of it had been written by Watty. His style was dry, pithy, emotion colouring the words until the reader was there in the homes of the tortured families.

All five cases had much in common. The murderer of each dead child had been convicted and sentenced to life imprisonment. There had never been an element of doubt. Appeals had been merely part of the process, indeed three

of the men freely admitted their guilt, the other two main-
taining a silence to hide other crimes of the same nature.

When she was back at her desk the phone trilled. It was
Gerry, calling to tell Sue of more information he had
gleaned for her.

'That's great. Can I collect it now?'

'Why not come to the flat about six? Stay on for dinner.'

'I'm very tempted, but what about Richard?'

'He'll only mind that he'll miss seeing you. He has to do
an extra theatre shift.'

Sue thought of Gerry's cooking. 'I'd love to come.'

'Would it help to talk about it?'

Sue looked up, startled.

'You've had something on your mind all evening. Can
I help?'

Gerry had been a marvellous host. His home, always
immaculate, had been welcoming with fresh flowers, flickering fire, good food. He had been undemanding company, she realized, not forcing her into brittle sociability.

'I'm sorry.'

'Don't be. Is it your pilgrimage?'

'What makes you think that?'

'I looked up the name Porter in hospital records. There
was only one in Burwell Close. I found a dead child.
I should say a murdered child.' Gerry kept his expression
carefully neutral. 'It must have been very distressing for
you, meeting her parents.'

There was no pressure on Sue to confide, no sense of
urgency, yet she could feel words bubbling up like tears
which needed to be shed.

'The list of names I showed you?'

'I remember.'

Sue bent to her bag, taking out the sheet she had
received from Stephen. Gerry took it from her and read, his
stillness conveying more horror than any outburst of
emotion.

'God rest their souls.'

It was said so quietly Sue could barely hear him.

'And Colin had been seeing these people?'

She nodded. 'He'd asked who knew they wanted the murderers dead.'

Gerry took off his glasses, polishing them while he thought. 'Did he find out?'

'I gather everyone did.'

'No one in particular?'

'Not one name.'

'Strange.' Gerry read through Stephen's information again. He looked at Sue. 'Colin was always so firmly against the idea capital punishment should return.'

'He was,' Sue agreed. 'So am I. It's completely barbaric to think of taking anyone's life like that.'

'Yes,' Gerry mused. 'I've heard you say so, both of you. Unlike many people, you genuinely meant it. Is it possible Colin had begun to change his mind?'

She frowned, trying to remember wisps in time. 'No, not Colin.'

'A catalogue like this,' Gerry said, tapping the paper with his glasses, 'it makes you realize the needs of the situation.'

Sue sat up, shocked. 'You don't agree with the "Bring back the rope" lobby?'

'No, I don't,' Gerry assured Sue earnestly, 'but there are those who do.' He held the list towards her. 'What did the parents tell you? Did any of them want the murderer of their child hanged?'

'They all did. The ones I saw.'

'Would they be better off with the killers dead?'

Gerry would expect a completely honest opinion. Lying back with her eyes closed Sue could see again Mrs Porter, the Cahills, Mrs McGovern. 'They are,' she sighed, defeated.

'I don't understand.'

Sue explained the deaths of the murderers.

'All of them?'

'Every one.'

He re-read the list. With Gerry's quick grasp of facts he must know the data by heart, Sue decided.

'Five. Out of the entire prison population it must be a very small percentage.'

'I've no doubt it is, but why did Colin concentrate on them?' Sue sat up restless, haunted. 'Gerry, I've just got this feeling that if I can solve that puzzle, I shall know why Colin died.'

'Perhaps then you would be able to rest,' he said gently.

Chapter Five

'With Bobby tied up, I should be getting his work.'

Sue looked up and met mutiny. Paula was a true West Sussex girl, tall, fine-boned, well-schooled, arrogant.

'His work?'

'The stories he's usually allocated. All I get are piddling little paras. Even then that stupid girl Beth hacks them to pieces and rewrites.'

Beth was sunny-faced and usually draped in a colourful rugby shirt. She was ruthless, but only when the copy she had to deal with demanded it. Paula had a lot to learn about writing for a London daily.

'It's called an apprenticeship,' Sue told her. 'There's nothing formal about it, but when those higher up the line think you're ready, you'll get your chances. There will always be someone like Beth to check on what you do.'

'Your copy doesn't get rewritten.'

'Maybe not so much now. I had to learn too.' The sweep of Sue's arm encompassed the huge room with its working journalists. 'We all did.'

Paula was not reconciled to the idea. 'I'm sitting twiddling my thumbs half the time, and having to listen to everyone bleat about "how hard Sue works". You could pass on some of your assignments.'

Sue sat up, her patience evaporating fast. 'I write what I'm asked to,' she told the younger girl, ice beginning to splinter her voice. 'The rest of the time I'm keeping myself familiar with current research. That way, when a story breaks suddenly, I've the data on it ready.'

'All that sort of stuff's in the computer, surely?'

'Who do you think puts it there? Besides, I've got my own notes, material I think important but too sensitive for public sight. It takes a lot of effort to build that up. If you've time on your hands, why don't you do the same?'

'I'm here to write, not hack,' Paula insisted. She had blonde hair perfectly cut to swing imperiously. Good features were marred, as they so often were, by a scowl darkening heavy-lashed eyes. 'It's time I had a crack at something worth writing about.'

'I don't hand out the assignments, you know that. Why haven't you been to see Sam Haddleston if you feel so strongly I'm in your way?'

A redness flushed up from Paula's throat, and she found it difficult to look at Sue who guessed that avenue had already been explored.

'Do I gather you've lobbied him?' Sue found it hard not to smile.

'He's a boor.'

'He's a first-rate newspaper man. If he thinks you can do a story, you'll get it, but you'll have to have your facts on tap, produce copy fast – and be prepared to have it sub-edited to fit the space allocated. When you're ready for that –'

'I'm not some damn trainee!'

Sue sat back in her chair and looked from the designer skirt of uncrushable wool up to the heavy cream silk shirt then to the haughty expression. Paula was right. She was a girl who had steamrollered her way through life. Learning was something she was not prepared to do.

'And it's your problem, not mine,' Sue said equably before turning to her keyboard and dismissing Paula from her thoughts.

A phone call brought a summons from Jepson. As Sue walked towards his office she wondered yet again why so much time and effort was being spent on products already set to disappear. Jepson's holdings included petrochemicals. Could there be competitors in that field? Other manufacturers trying to escape the ban and make oodles of cash in the process? It would explain a lot. Faye, Jepson's secretary, stood as Sue approached. Middle-aged and in respectable navy, she beckoned Sue to hurry, opening the door of the spacious sanctum redolent of good leather, expensive cigars, the modern hallmarks of wealth and power.

Sue doubted Jepson had had a good night. His eyes were pink-rimmed, his temper foul.

'Well?'

She related the latest research findings on nonyl phenols, depressing the huge man behind the wide slab of teak he called a desk. He pursed his fleshy lips, making his jowls wobble.

'So, only bad news.'

'Not if you live in Denmark.'

A growl demanded an explanation.

'Twenty-eight organic farmers in Denmark. They've got sperm counts well above the average,' Sue informed him.

'I hope you're not suggesting I wear bloody sandals and puddle around in manure!'

It seemed a good idea, but Sue kept a straight face, and her thoughts to herself. 'You could do, but it would make more sense if you kept away from foods rich in pesticides. They are what's decimated bird populations in this country by preventing them breeding.'

Jepson lay back in the squashy black leather of his chair. He surveyed Sue through narrowed eyes. A vestige of a smile appeared. 'No alligators, no chicken. What about pheasant?'

She cocked her head to one side, thinking. 'Possibly, especially from Scotland. Heather up there would be fairly well isolated from cultivated areas, so low levels of pesticide. Grouse, as well. Probably any Scottish game bird would do.'

'Denmark or Scotland. That's my choice?'

She shrugged her shoulders. 'Either would have low stress levels, unless you get frustrated with the quiet life,' she grinned.

'Get out of here!' he bellowed, and Sue departed.

Bobby was hovering, the long sleeves of his shirt neatened by ornate elastic, similar to the silver arm bands Jepson favoured. 'Anything I should know?'

'I don't think so. He just felt like barking a bit. I'd guess a headache caused by inflamed meninges.'

Bobby frowned.

'Hangover,' Sue explained and went away quickly.

Kate and Clive had their heads together, planning something devious. Sue hoped the target would not take it too badly. If it was Bobby, he would probably throw a tantrum. After telling Sally she would be working at home later, Sue stocked herself up with spare disks and headed for her car.

'Poppet!' Mr Lavin was in the garden, tying up shrubs which had been torn by winter winds. He hugged Sue, and she felt his strength, smelled the goodness of cold, clean skin. 'Staying long?'

'Not really,' she said, concerned to see disappointment flare briefly in his eyes before he smiled.

'Never mind. We'll go and see what your mother has for lunch. We've been a bit concerned, because we couldn't ring you. Fortunately, your mother had Pippa's number and she reassured us. Something about a broken phone?'

'Help! You've reminded me. I must get a new one. Modern plastic doesn't do too well against Victorian tiles. I discovered that when the old one dropped off the mantelpiece on to the hearth. I've still got my mobile from the *Journal*, so I haven't felt too cut off.'

'Of course! I forgot about that number. Never mind. You're OK, and you're here.'

To be wrapped in the undemanding warmth of her old home soothed Sue. Since her return to work she had kept herself more occupied than ever, and was very tired. After lunch it was tempting to sit comfortably and let consciousness recede, but she pushed the idea away. The price for rest and oblivion was too high, the dreams that ended them harrowing.

'Dad, the disks you've been looking after, I need to take them back with me.'

'Of course. I'll get them.'

'Do you have to go back?' Mrs Lavin wanted to know.

''Fraid so, Mum. I need my job, and unless I look after it, someone will sneak in under and swipe it.' Paula for one, and perhaps Bobby. She wondered just what Kate and Clive were planning for Bobby.

Her mother sighed. 'I know you love what you do, darling, but it does all seem rather cut-throat.'

'Not really. I'm safe – as long as I go on producing good copy. At least I can be flexible about working in the office. It means I can come here occasionally and get fed properly.'

'That reminds me, I've liver and bacon ready for your freezer.'

'Mum!' Sue protested, laughing. 'I can only just shut the door now.'

'You need iron, darling, and you must eat,' Mrs Lavin urged.

'I do. Pippa and Ken are conspiring to feed me at every turn. In fact,' she said confidentially, 'I think I might be the means of those two becoming an item.'

'Pippa and Colin's friend?' Mrs Lavin was intrigued. 'What makes you think so?' she asked, settling down for a good gossip.

Back in her flat, Sue found copying disks a long, boring

job. While data was transferred and saved, she tidied papers, washed bedlinen, cleaned kitchen surfaces. Night became very early morning, but still she persisted, determined to have a set of information which could be stored safely, away from possible predators.

It was the exhausted loss of senses rather than rewarding sleep which claimed her, but it sufficed and she ran to the car next morning, heading for Wapping in unexpected sunshine.

The vast *Journal* office had an end of term feel to it, laughter mixed more readily than usual with the purposeful movements of work. Maybe it was the brightness outside making smiles the order of the day, Sue decided.

Kate headed in her direction, red hair bouffant.

'Our lord and master has jetted off to sunnier climes,' Kate informed Sue as she settled at her desk.

'Perhaps he needs a holiday after working so hard,' she said, her mind not really on office gossip.

'Then why hasn't he taken Mrs Jepson? If anyone needs a break she certainly does, poor old cow.'

Sue looked up at Kate and smiled sweetly. 'If he's gone without her, she's getting it.'

Kate nodded approval, but before she could say anything, the phone rang. Sam Haddleston wanted to talk to Sue in his office. It was not a large room, but efficiently organized, the man at the desk broad, tough, uncompromising, fair curly hair crisply cut.

'This bug, *Helicobacter pylori*.' Sam looked up from an opened file, a pencil grasped firmly in strong fingers.

'What about it?'

'That's what I want to know.'

'A bacterium thought to be the cause of most gastric ulcers. Recent research suggests three out of four men suffering heart problems have the infection. A specific antibiotic has been developed to counteract it. We ran a piece yesterday about a case in which the antibiotic not only stopped the infection, it appeared to reverse an early stomach cancer.'

'Superbug?'

Sue grinned at him. 'It'll do for a headline. Mind you, it has to be pretty tough. Any organism that can float around safely in the high acidity of the stomach, it must be special.'

His eyes warmed in a quick smile. They were blue, she noticed. '500 words, Sue. Soon as you can.'

Several phone calls later Sue had the basis of her article. Quickly typed and entered, it was not long before she had Sam's approval. For some reason Beth was unavailable and it was Sam who suggested amendments to fill the available space.

Minor tasks presented themselves and were being dealt with when Paula sailed towards Sue, Beth a plump tug clad in jeans and the inevitable rugby shirt to the stern.

'You're supposed to be the expert,' Paula exploded. 'Check my copy and see what this imbecile has done to it.'

Beth, a cherubic expression on her rounded features, handed Sue a sheet of paper well-decorated with the blue stripes of erasures. Sue read, quickly, carefully. A white blackbird had been photographed in someone's garden. Paula had written it up in a high-flown style which owed more to romantic poets than science.

'You do realize it won't live long,' Sue warned. 'Too easily spotted by birds of prey and cats. It's why any white bird's so very rare, there's no chance of them breeding.'

'That's far too scientific for our readers,' Paula said dismissively. 'They wouldn't understand the premise.'

'You patronize them at your peril,' Sue told her. 'As for Beth's subbing, it's what she'd do if I handed that in.'

Beth grinned, her eyes merry. She went off with the copy without rubbing in Paula's defeat.

'You could have backed me up,' Paula said.

Sue could just see her at school. It would have been an expensive one, and Paula must have delighted in terrifying the small girls in their dorms.

'It's the job of the sub-editors to turn what we write into what can be printed. Try working with them, instead of taking every alteration as a slap in the face.'

'Why do we have to get that stupid Beth female?'

'Because she's good at doing what she's paid for, and because she's not stupid, far from it. Don't be misled by her "I'm just a poor old thing from the country" bit. She was born and bred in Hampstead and her grandfather owns chunks of Notting Hill – the expensive end.'

Paula was silenced, wondering why anyone should play down their antecedents in such a way. 'Why does she do it?'

'Originally, to be taken seriously by the print boys. Now, it's a habit. It amuses her to see how people react to the yokel bit.'

Sue saw Paula flush, no doubt remembering cutting remarks in the past which had been answered by one of Beth's broad smiles.

Kate appeared over the top of Sue's terminal. 'Have you seen Watty's new spread? It's a bit basic.' She drifted off again, heading for the diarist, Cary Mitchell, and two of his blonde assistants.

Sue beckoned a messenger, asking for a copy of the layout. She spread it on her desk. Under the single word 'Punishment', was a shot of bare buttocks, the stripes of a beating ruler-straight in swollen and discoloured flesh. Across the head and shoulders of the body were the words 'Crime – Vandalism'. Sue's eyes roved quickly over the other photographs on the sheet. A young girl looked back at her, beauty crisscrossed with the zipper marks of hundreds of stitches. At the bottom of the photo was the caption 'Crime – None'.

The theme was repeated with chilling monotony. A scene of a tiny coffin borne from church by grieving relatives. A man in a hospital bed, wired, drip-fed, his head swathed in bandages. An elderly man cowering, afraid, the medals on his chest won in a cleaner war. An old person, features so distorted by a beating it was impossible to tell if it had been male or female before becoming a victim. Body bags, filled but shapeless, next to an exploded car. Under each was the same message. 'Crime – None'. Watty had asked a question in the last line of the sheet. 'Which country is barbaric?'

Sue went to find Watty. He was getting himself coffee from a machine, looking mournfully at the depressing brown liquid which emerged.

'Will it do, lass?' He nodded at the layout.

'And how! Did Jepson see it before he went?'

'No way! With the old bastard off chasing some totty, I thought I'd try it out. Sam's given it the OK, and with luck, the new girlfriend will keep Jeppers away from finding out until after we go to press.'

Sue looked up at Watty, smiling. 'He needs all the rest he can get. He had a hell of a headache when I saw him yesterday.'

'Couldn't happen to a nicer chap,' Watty grinned and pointed to his article with pride. 'I've been trying to get that past him for a long while now.'

'You've got a thing about helping victims, haven't you?'

'Someone's got to do it.'

'I thought our legislators were supposed to.'

'Huh!' he snorted, pouring the despised coffee away. 'All they could come up with was the Criminal Justice Act. It means the criminals are the only ones to get justice. Some justice! Keep the bastards in circulation and make more money for all the bloody lawyers. Now if there was a Victims' Justice Act we might be getting somewhere.'

Sue thought of Colin and the unknown assailant. 'Amen to that,' she said softly.

'I'm sorry, lass. I wasn't thinking.'

'No, you're right. How about standing for Parliament and getting the bill through?'

Peals of deep laughter expressed what Watty thought of that idea. 'No,' he said at last, 'I'll just stay where I am, dealing with honest criminals, and nagging Jepson's conscience.'

'He's got one? When he's away cheating on Mrs J?'

'With his bimbo, you mean?'

Sue nodded.

'Let's hope they both get what they want out of it,' Watty said cynically, 'though I can't quite see her providing him with the son and heir he's desperate to acquire.'

'Jepson? But he's an old man!'

'Enough of that, thank you. He's ages wi' me.'

Watty took her arm and they headed back to work.

'I just can't see him changing a nappy,' Sue decided.

'It's not that part of being a father he's anxious to practise,' Watty laughed. 'Why the hell do you think he's been so keen on this campaign you're running for him?'

Sue stopped, turning to look at Watty. 'Public interest – which roughly translated means increased readership, and lots more lolly?'

'That, too. No, the last two bimbos he shacked up with didn't get pregnant. He's worried it might be his fault.'

Sue frowned. 'You're serious, aren't you? He's got me chasing fertility research, just so he can play Daddy?'

'It's his paper.' Watty leaned forward and tapped the crime and punishment article with the stem of his pipe. 'You and I – and Sam – might think this a more important crusade.'

'He wants a son so badly?'

'Aye, he does, lass. It's an obsession.'

'This campaign, all the work, the cash for Maginty's, that's what it's for? To help Jepson get a girlfriend pregnant?'

'It's likely. Mind, he probably convinced himself he was doing it for the Great British Public.'

'And I thought it might be to do down a business competitor.'

'Knowing Jepson, it's probably been helping there as well. But listen, don't understimate the effect of sterility on a man, any man. So Jepson's powerful. He can buy help from the best specialists. Failing that he can take his frustration out on his enemies – or us,' Watty grinned. 'No, this campaign of yours could do some good. It might help poor little sods with no hope.'

Sue was silent a moment, remembering past conversations. 'My granny used to talk of men in her village, pathetic souls whose only attribute was that they could sire children. Without that, she would say, they were less than nothing.'

'You've just described the present day no-hoper.'

'The ones who turn to crime because no girl will ever have their baby? Perhaps it's the curse of all this modern civilization we keep hearing about?'

'Modern?' Watty looked, unseeing, past Sue's shoulder, his thoughts somewhere familiar, pleasant. 'Lord, how long shall the wicked triumph?' he quoted softly. 'How long shall they utter and speak hard things, and all the workers of iniquity boast themselves? They break in pieces thy people, O Lord, and afflict thine heritage. They slay the widow and the stranger, and murder the fatherless.' He stood up, shaking his head, as though to clear a miasma. 'Modern, my bloody foot. It was a curse more than two thousand years ago.'

'You'd think, in all that time, someone would have found the answer.'

'Judgement shall return to the righteous,' Watty boomed suddenly, 'and all the upright in heart shall follow them.'

'Not again!' It was Kate, elegant today in dark jade green which made the flame of her hair seem brighter. 'Did you have to learn the whole of the Bible when you sat in short trousers in your chapel? We've certainly had most of it thrown at us over the years.'

'It was a kirk, and you're still a pagan bitch,' Watty informed her cheerfully.

With her office chores complete, Sue went shopping for a

new phone, carrying her bulging briefcase to her bank and the privacy of a safety deposit box for her disks.

She was just leaving the bank when the mobile phone trilled, earning her a look of disgust and envy from a shaven-headed girl, dirty in old denim. A stream of abuse followed Sue as she sought a quiet corner for her conversation.

'Stephen Childs, Sue. Can you meet me this evening? About six?'

'You've got something?' Her eagerness must sound pathetic, she decided. 'Have you got a copy of the video?'

'No. But I know where there is one. It's being delivered to a processing lab in Soho. There's a wine bar in Dean Street. I can't remember the name, but it's French. It's not far from the turning to Old Compton Street.'

'I'll find it.'

Sue spent the intervening hours at home, installing the phone, eating some of her mother's food. Pippa arrived for a chat, a Pippa with a new radiance to her skin and an aura of happiness. There was no need for Sue to guess why. Pippa's frequent use of Ken's name revealed the source of her joy.

At six Sue hoped she was in the right place, the Soho bar noisy, bustling.

'On the dot. Thanks for coming.' Stephen sat next to her. 'I won't keep you long.'

'Did you get it?'

'The video?'

She nodded, her eyes wide with apprehension.

'In a way,' he said. 'Fortunately, since it was to be part of an inquiry, the technician dealing with the security cameras made a copy off his own bat. He's loaned me that. It won't go through the books.'

'Have you seen it?'

'Yes.'

'Can I see it?'

'Best not.' His voice was gentle.

'Why?' Sue's chin was mutinous.

'I don't recommend it.' Stephen's face was bleak, his eyes shuttered. He reached into an inside pocket and withdrew a photograph. 'It's a bit grainy. The definition's as good as it could be, under the circumstances.'

He handed the print to Sue. She looked at it, frowning, seeing the head and one shoulder of a man in a crowd. He was dark, burly, in workman's clothes, a light-coloured woolly hat obscuring any sign of hair. The background had been sliced away from the man's right.

'Is he the one?' she wanted to know.

'He was nearest to your husband just before he fell.'

'Could Colin have been pushed? Please. I need to know.'

'There's no conclusive proof on the video – but yes, I think it's possible he was.'

'And this man did it?'

Sue looked hard at the picture, trying to link it in her memory with anyone she had encountered before.

'It's a distinct possibility. That's as far as I'm prepared to go.'

'Can I keep it?'

'If you're sure you want to.'

'I'm sure.' She tucked it safely in her handbag, slipping her head through the strap so that she wore the bag tourist-fashion.

'You won't try finding him, will you?'

'Why not?'

'We don't know who he is. More importantly, we don't know who's behind him. Look,' he said, suddenly earnest. 'I'm owed a few favours. I'll get copies of the photo circulated where they'll do most good, if, I repeat if, you leave well alone.'

Sue made no promises. 'Was there anything to help you on the video? Anything at all?'

Stephen hesitated.

'You recognized someone?' Sue said.

'Yes, but then the kind of guy we get to arrest uses the tube too.'

'He's not connected?'

'To your husband's death? Hardly likely.'

A waitress came to clear empty glasses. 'Will you be eating?' she wanted to know, her Australian accent crisp.

'Yes,' Stephen decided, looking at the menu written in chalk on a large blackboard. 'What do you fancy?' he asked Sue.

She thought, head tilted to one side. 'A croque monsieur, with a side salad – and mineral water.'

Stephen opted for a ham and cheese omelette.

'What about your girlfriend?'

'Louise?'

'Won't she be expecting you?'

'She's at a working dinner and I go on duty in an hour.'

'Tell me about her.'

Stephen's expression softened. He looked younger, more vulnerable as he talked of the woman with whom he shared his life.

'How did you come to meet?' Sue asked.

'She was a witness – of sorts, in a case of mine.' His eyes darkened. 'It almost got her killed. Now,' he went on, 'I keep her as far away from my work as possible.'

Sue laughed. 'Does that mean me?'

He nodded, suddenly grim. 'Louise is psychic. Out of the blue she gets an image, perhaps a sudden feeling of terror. Once, she held the photo of a man and heard children crying. She described the sound as desolate. Then one by one the children stopped. We found the bodies in his garden.'

Sue shivered. 'It must be hell for her.'

'It is. Other people's misery tears her apart.'

'I'd like to meet her one day, but you're right. Not yet.'

They finished their meal and Stephen rose to leave. 'Where've you parked your car?'

'In the multi-storey, just round the corner – but I'm not going straight home. Since I'm here, I'll get some Christmas presents. There's a favourite shop of mine, full of Chinese imports. I always find something.'

*   *   *

Sue headed for her car at last, two bulging bags full of well-packed china. A sari shop caught her eye, the colours of the silks tempting. Once inside she was seduced by the aroma of sandalwood, the grace of the sales lady, business-like but charming in a dark red sari under a very British navy wool cardigan. Packet after packet of glowing silk was spread before Sue. One, spring green with an intri-cately patterned hem of gold, made her see Pippa. She smiled. Pippa might not wear it Indian-style, but the fabric would add a touch of colour to her flat.

While the gift was being wrapped, Sue wandered around. Midnight blue silk, edged with silver. She could just see her mother in a long-skirted suit made from it. No Asian swathing for Mum, Sue thought. It would become an addition to her wardrobe in a style appropriate for the social life of Dorking.

Christmas, Sue reflected, as she drove home through streets crowded with traffic, shoppers, it had to be faced. The day itself would be filled by her parents, church, lunch, television. It was twenty-four hours to get through. What would Mrs Willoughby advise, Sue wondered? Per-haps she might go and see her. It would help break the pattern set by other, happier Christmases.

She recognized Ken's car parked outside the house. Pippa would be busy this evening. Sue sighed. While she was glad Pippa and Ken were happy together, Sue did miss her friend's visits, the lazing on the couch with a fresh cup of coffee, the hours of peaceful gossip.

'I'm just jealous,' she informed the steering wheel. Had Pippa envied her with Colin? It had never seemed so.

Sue picked up her handbag, remembering the photo it contained. Stephen had promised to try and identify the man. Who was he?

Did he hate Colin because of some past case, a grudge maybe? Or had he been paid to end the life of a stranger?

As she fitted her key into the lock, Sue asked herself for the thousandth time, why Colin had been taken away from her. The trail through the dead murderers was cold, and yet she sensed it affected her somehow. She must find the link, then she could rest.

Standing in the hall Sue instinctively sniffed. Only the very faint aroma of pot pourri from the bowl on the table was detectable. Muscles sagged a little as she realized she was safe and in her own home. Tears rose and threatened composure, but it was reaction to tiredness, a self-pity which was not grief for a sleeping Colin.

As she went through the main door of the *Journal* building next morning, Sue became aware of stifled giggles. For most of the week large posters had been prominently displayed, showing the before and after effects of nonyl phenols. A group of clerks were hiding one such exhibit. She frowned, trying to remember. It had been two shots of a pool. The first, taken some years ago, showed the water teeming with alligators. The most recent had the water smooth, clear, the absence of the huge reptiles tragic.

The giggles moved towards the lifts and Sue could see what had happened. The 'before' picture had been changed to one of Arnold Schwarzenegger bare, bronzed, beefy. Its counterpart was a lifesize study of Bobby Chalmers, complete with red braces and silver arm bands, the comparison obvious, cruel.

'This had better come down,' Sue said to a security officer hovering with a wide grin.

'It was Mr Chalmers said he was in charge of this lot. We could only take it down when he gave the say so.'

Sue's mouth tightened grimly. 'Get rid of it. Now!'

She turned and met Bobby's accusing eyes. He had just arrived and stood rooted to the welcoming mat inside the huge swing doors.

'Mr Chalmers agrees with me. It's got to go,' she informed the guard.

'If you say so, mam. Pity. It's a good likeness – of Arnie.' He heaved away the offending cardboard.

Bobby was nearly in tears, his full lower lip trembling.

Sue went to him. 'Come on. Get your head up and get into that office with a smile on your face. Thank the whole lot of them for the publicity.'

'It's so unfair –'

'Fair! You expect fair? For God's sake, you're a journalist!'

'But we're scientists, you and me. We're different.'

She looked down at the dejected boy. 'No, Bobby. We're just like everyone else. We get hurt. We get going. If we've got the guts, we finish the job. If we haven't –' Sue shrugged her shoulders.

He looked up at her, searching her face for sincerity. 'You should know,' he sighed before heading for the lift.

'A bit much?' Sue asked Kate later.

'Do you think so, darling? You didn't see him trying to take advantage of your enforced absence to wheedle his way into Jepson's good books and your job. It was almost bad enough for party politics. Sam was furious with Bobby. As for Watty he was ready to exterminate the little tick.'

Sue was aghast. 'I thought Bobby had upset you and Clive.'

'He had, darling, but you made a much better excuse.'

Watty made a triumphal entry. The spread on crime and punishment had taken over the whole front page. All the breakfast television channels had featured it.

'What price your bloody hormones now?' Watty demanded of Sue, his grin wide.

'Suitably in retreat,' she laughed. 'Seriously, though, I'm glad. Your layout said what needed saying.'

'And sold a few more papers, too,' Watty added, tapping the side of his nose knowingly. 'When old buggerlugs comes back, I'll be able to quote him chapter and verse of increased sales. It's the only thing he understands – after you-know-what.'

'Where is he, anyway?'

'Cannes, Nice. Somewhere French and fancy, where it's too hot for bimbos to wear clothes. Just think of what the sight of all that bare female flesh will do to his libido! Still, he's got to get his testosterone on parade somehow, I suppose. You're a scientist, Sue. Are oysters in season?'

'At a price.'

'He'll pay.'

'He could pick up hepatitis A from them.'

'Could he, indeed? Now, there's a thought,' Watty said with relish.

The few days left before Christmas passed in a blur. Sue kept Bobby as busy as possible, and passed over to Paula small items for checking and writing. The discipline of shaping facts in a hundred words or so would be good practice for the ambitious girl. It should keep at bay her penchant for lurching into a mess of adjectives.

Pippa was staying in Islington, Ken keeping her company over the holiday. Sue had watched the relationship grow, become solid. It had meant she had less of Pippa's company, but to see her friend glowing with happiness lightened her own dark hours.

On Christmas Eve Sue carried a box of Christmas tree decorations upstairs. 'Please, use them if you can.'

'Are you sure?' Pippa's eyes were concerned, anxious her own joy did not make Sue's day harder.

'My mother has glass balls that were kept safe all through the war. If I took this modern stuff home it would be regarded as outright blasphemy.'

Ken looked younger, more carefree. 'Come on, you can help me decorate the tree while Pippa makes us coffee.'

It was pleasant in the warm room. Pippa had left the wooden floors bare, sealing and polishing them to give an illusion of space, but Sue could see a squash racquet, files, traces of Ken's occupancy. She wondered how long it would be before the move was permanent.

'Finished your shopping?' Sue asked.

'I was going to get some food later on.' Pippa stretched lazily. 'Ken's stocked us up with wine so we shan't suffer if I forget.'

Sue insisted on emptying her freezer and filling Pippa's. Ken helped carry the packages so carefully labelled by Sue's mother but there was not enough room.

'That settles it,' Pippa decided. 'I know it's early, but you're staying for dinner to help us eat what won't go in.'

It was a happy evening, the mixture of foods providing reasons for laughter. Sue and Ken took over the washing up while Pippa restored order.

'Any news from Stephen?' she asked him as Pippa sorted out the fridge.

'None, I'm afraid. It's an all-out police effort since that witness in the Astwood murder trial was shot.'

'That was dreadful,' Pippa exclaimed. 'What are his chances?'

'Of surviving, not bad. Of giving evidence? Well, would you after getting a message like that?' Ken knew what it was like to lie in hospital with bullet wounds.

'Astwood. Isn't he the one who killed a policeman?' Sue checked.

'Chas Harley.' Ken's mouth was a thin line of gravity. 'I knew him. We were at Hendon together.'

There was a silence, a mourning in the quietness.

'It looks as though Astwood will get off. The worst thing,' Ken went on, 'is that it will make any copper's chance of getting killed that much more likely. It will devalue them, and they're low enough already on the scale of priorities.'

'Oh no,' Sue said quickly, 'surely not.'

'No?' Ken sounded bitter. 'If I go out and kill a policeman, I am taking the whole of his life away. Should I be caught and convicted, the law only allows part of my life to be spent in jail.'

Pippa looked puzzled.

Ken prepared to explain. 'Imagine the policeman had another forty years of life due. If I spend twenty in jail, his life is only worth half of mine. I'm more valuable than he is.'

'I see what you mean,' Pippa agreed.

'And if the killer walks free, it makes the policeman's life of no value at all by comparison,' Sue said slowly. She thought of the parents of dead children she had talked to, their anger, their bitterness. 'And a child's life?'

'Then the equation becomes obscene,' Ken said with quiet passion.

'It's not surprising child-killers get a hard time in prison,' Pippa said.

'Left in the community, they'd be lynched,' Ken told the girls.

'I shall be if I don't get my packing done and go home,' Sue laughed. 'Mum was expecting me hours ago.'

Sue was about to leave when she remembered she had not sorted out which disks she planned to take. It would be cumbersome and unnecessary to take them all, so she began to go through them, flicking the occasional one into her computer to check how much space was left. Nearly finished, she pushed in a disk and watched the screen. Not enough bytes to make it worth taking. Placing it on the pile of discards, Sue was about to pick up the next when she frowned. There had been something wrong with the last disk's directory. She looked at the label. 'Genetic diseases and DNA.' Back in the machine, the list of files appeared. They were all as she expected. What was it that puzzled her?

Sue sat back in her chair trying to make sense of a riddle with no shape. Annoyed with herself she got up and closed her suitcase, counted the plastic bags of presents and went back to the screen. What was it? She remembered her father's advice. When there no obvious explanation, be methodical. Sighing, she began to add up the bytes used by the files, subtracting the total. That was it! It did not tally with the number still available. A very large file had not been entered, it must be in limbo.

A sense of excitement invaded Sue. She automatically labelled all her files. It could only have been Colin who had used the space. It must have been his way of hiding information, storing it where it would be difficult to find. The file would need a password, but she had no clue as to what it might be.

She tried every possible combination of his initials, hers, their names, dates, all to no avail. Restless, Sue paced round the flat, straightening the duvet flattened by her luggage. She closed the drawer of her bedside table.

'That's it,' she cried. The four letters on the back of the list of names and addresses. She hurried back to the machine. R M L C she entered. Nothing. Sue closed her eyes, picturing the lunch with Gerry. His kindly face with its shining, gold-rimmed glasses was there in her mind's eye. She heard his voice again as he wondered about the first letter. P or R, he had mused. P M L C Sue typed in, and waited. The beginning of the file appeared. She saw a list of names and addresses. After it Colin had recorded his own researches, then added his thoughts, his fears.

Sue read his words. He had written simply, lucidly, and she learned of a secret group, its methods ending in death.

Convinced that finding out what had obsessed Colin in his last weeks would help her understand why he had died made Sue look at the name at the top of the list. This man would tell her, she decided. Whatever it took, she would have the answer.

Sue no longer knew or cared if the tears rising in her were of grief or fury. She linked the computer to her printer and as the paper was fed through and used, she phoned her mother.

'Mum? I'll be late, I'm afraid. Something's come up.'

Chapter Six

Sue's anger did not abate as she drove into deepest Sussex. Once more she was starting with a catalogue of names, some of them known to her, but this was no pilgrimage. Someone in the group must have been aware of Colin's interest in them, and had organized the fatal push from the crowded platform. The possibility that any of those named might have callously decided on Colin's death caused Sue to put aside her grief. She allowed the heat of her emotions to burn away at the ice inside her.

Before leaving Islington Sue had made two more copies of the file, stopping on the way to post one of them. She was barely aware of the route she chose, going through Colin's words on the disk over and over again. Why had he not confided in her? He knew she could keep a secret, none better. Tears obscured a long stretch of dual carriageway. Why had he not trusted her?

When Sue reached the village of the address, she had to ask for directions from a man, swaddled against the cold, walking his dog.

'Keep on the way you're going. It's second right, but you've got to watch out – the road narrows down to a lane. Keep on till you see a fork in the road. The left one's the drive of the house you're looking for. Hope you enjoy the party,' he called out after her.

She let out the clutch and moved away. Little did he know, Sue thought grimly. If she had her way it would be one hell of a party.

Only when she took the left fork on to a driveway did

Sue realize why the man had laughed. At the end of the drive was a gem of a house, old enough to have earned the label Elizabethan. In the floodlights illuminating the facade, she could see the deep rose of the bricks, the mullioned windows, iron-studded doorways. Up into the darkness soared chimneys, the tops hidden by the night. Lights glowed from all the downstairs windows, and she could hear music.

Parking was not easy, cars lining the gravel approach. Bitterness made Sue press the accelerator so savagely that small stones spurted from her wheels to strike the glossy limousines alongside. She braked by the front door, oblivious to the needs of others, and marched to the bell pull. It was solid, iron, imposing, one wrench enough to send the message. The door was opened by a butler, the professional smile deserting him when he realized Sue was in jeans and a thick sweater.

'I want to see Martin Lawrence,' she demanded.

From a great height the manservant surveyed Sue along the length of a narrow nose. Slowly he progressed from her boots to her hair. 'Mister Lawrence is not at home.'

She laughed, the sound harsh with disbelief. 'I doubt he would leave all his guests unattended. Tell him the widow of Colin Bennett is here to see him.'

The man bent a fraction, the bow insulting. 'One may regret your loss, madam, but Mister Lawrence is not at home – to the widow of Colin Bennett.'

The insolence of his last remark made Sue's temper flare.

'I'd better warn you that I am also a journalist. If I do not see Lawrence within the next five minutes, his extra-curricular activities will be spread all over the daily papers. I'll include the information that it was because his doorman refused me entry. Will he approve of you for that? Or will you be sacked?'

The man did not seem quite so tall, and his cheeks reddened. 'Wait there.'

Sue looked at her watch. 'You've got three minutes to get

him here, then I'm off.' She went back to her car, starting the engine violently so that it could be heard she was ready to leave quickly.

With thirty seconds to spare the front door was opened again and the manservant hurried to her. 'Mister Lawrence will see you.'

Switching off the engine Sue sat for a moment. She drew in a deep, calming breath, then got out and marched into the house.

Waiting for her in a small panelled room was Martin Lawrence, grey-haired and elegant in evening dress.

'Mrs Bennett. How may I help you?' He was tall, handsome, urbane.

Sue thrust at him the computer print-out she had brought so quickly from London. 'Is it true?'

He glanced at the sheets, riffling them to check their contents. Although his features were implacable, Sue fancied she saw a muscle flicker at the corner of his mouth.

'Is what true?' he said at last, his eyes wary.

'That you head a group which selects and executes convicted murderers.'

His nostrils flared as he inhaled air carefully. 'Not quite. Please. Do sit down.'

Sue's expression was stormy, niceties not part of her confrontation.

'If you do, I can,' he explained, 'and I've had rather a tiring day.' The tone of his voice was one which could seduce a jury to order. 'Please. We need to discuss this.'

Sue sat on the nearest chair, refusing to relax against the padding, while Martin Lawrence lifted one narrow knee over the other and twitched the immaculate wool of his dress trousers to neatness. As a QC he was used to arguing on his feet, prosecuting for the crown in wig and gown. Now he must plead his case in the comfort of his own home.

'How did you find this?' he asked, gesturing to the list.

'It was on one of my disks.'

'Was it, now?' He seemed surprised. 'Which one?'

'Genetic diseases. That file was in limbo.'

'I don't understand.'

'It had no title, so it would have been missed. You would have needed a password.'

'Ah, a password. And it was?'

'The letters P C M L.'

Martin Lawrence pondered a moment, then his face cleared. 'Of course. I was prosecuting counsel in each of the cases your husband listed.'

'So, why did you have him killed?' There was a plea for the truth mixed in with the anger of the question.

'My dear Mrs Bennett!' Martin Lawrence appeared genuinely shocked. 'I can assure you the last thing we wanted was Colin dead. Apart from the fact we knew him well, and liked him enormously, his accident was extremely embarrassing for us. We had no idea what information he had left behind.'

'And that was why you had my home burgled?'

He nodded, his expression apologetic. 'I'm afraid we needed to be sure. Your friends insisted everything was carried out as discreetly as possible.'

'My friends?'

'There was great concern for you. They did not want you upset.'

'My phone's bugged, my home robbed, and I'm not supposed to be upset? At least I understand now how the burglar got in. Bill Farnham gave him Colin's spare keys, didn't he?'

'Mrs Bennett, please believe me, you were very much our concern. It was important to know if Colin had left any evidence which could lead back to us. I can assure you only one person checked the tapes from the phone tap, and he made sure they were destroyed immediately they ceased to be of use.'

'Was it Bill Farnham?'

'No. As you guessed, it was Bill who obtained the keys for us. He was anxious there should be no damage.' Martin

Lawrence bent towards Sue, his expression earnest, kindly. 'We wanted your home disturbed as little as possible.'

'You wanted? Who the hell do you think you are?'

'Let me explain.'

'You're nothing but a bunch of criminal lunatics.' Sue was desperately near to tears of rage. 'Colin's dead because of you. I don't know why I'm so sure, but I am. Hadn't you better save your explanations for the police?'

'At least when Colin talked with us, he was more rational. He understood no prosecution was possible.'

'Colin talked to you? When?'

'Let me see. Six weeks, more. Perhaps two months before the accident.'

Sue tried to remember what Colin had been like two months before he died. Autumn. He had been happy, carefree. Had these men let him wait to die?

'You arrange deaths – and now he's dead. Why should I not hold you responsible?'

'Cause and effect there may be in this situation, but we were not the cause of him dying.'

'I find that hard to believe.'

'Naturally, but you're a scientist as well as a journalist. You know only too well that many truths are difficult to absorb.'

Sue was immobile, her fury spent, beaten out against a wall of words.

Martin Lawrence realized her exhaustion. 'You have only glimpsed the outline of our aims,' he said gently. 'Perhaps you will allow me to say a little about what we do.' He took her stillness for assent. 'When there is a problem in today's society, social workers are called in. They have a case conference to discuss all the facts, then they decide on appropriate action. Sometimes that will smash families apart for ever, destroy the happiness of children all in the name of what is best.'

'And you think of yourselves as social workers? Don't be so ridiculous.'

'You are quite right, we're not. Everyone mentioned by

Colin in his file is very well qualified in their own field. We number doctors and psychiatrists, as well as experienced solicitors and counsel. Take a careful look at the file when you have time. I presume you have a copy?'

Sue smiled grimly: 'One at home, and one in the post.'

'You came prepared.' Martin Lawrence smiled. 'I like that. It shows commendable sense. I understand you've been visiting some of the families of those poor children.'

'How do you know?'

'One of our number, not listed here, by the way, keeps in contact with the relatives. Fortunately, you were not recognized as a journalist, and your visits gave the families great comfort.'

'You take your social work seriously.' Sue's voice conveyed her cynicism.

'Of course. The ravages caused in a family by the brutal loss of a child should never be taken lightly. For the general public it is something to stir emotions over the cornflakes for a day or two, but for those who loved the child, the agony never goes away.'

Sue was silent, remembering the homes she had visited. 'How did you do it? The executions?'

'If that is how you must phrase it. In the aftermath of a child's murder we would be notified as to the emotional state of the parents and siblings. At a meeting we would review all the options. As long as there was no doubt at all about the guilt of the convicted person, we would estimate if his demise was of real benefit to the family. In other words, would they be able to get on with their shattered lives better if the monster was dead.' He leaned towards Sue. 'You met them. Had it helped?'

She thought of Mrs Porter in Whitechapel, the Cahills daily seeing the park where their daughter died, Mrs McGovern in Glasgow with half her twins gone. Every one had felt relief, a new sense of purpose when their child's killer was dead.

'Yes. None of them wished any of the men to live.' She frowned. 'I still don't see how you did it.'

106

'We took no positive steps, once the decision was made. Each of those murderers is at risk the second they set foot in jail after the trial. The prison services go to great lengths to keep them in reasonable health. In some cases, we simply recommended to suitably placed individuals the protection should not be quite so all-embracing.'

'The suicide?'

'If Hopkins chose to die that way, why should he be stopped?'

'The heart attack. Natural causes?' Sue said cynically.

'Ah. As you know, some of our members are medical men. They have friends in the prison service. Doctors are busy men and women. They cannot always get to a patient in time.'

Sue shuddered. 'The murder in Barlinnie, was that planned?'

'Not by us. You must understand, Mrs Bennett, any prisoner who despatches a child-murderer becomes a hero to the other inmates. It's a question of who gets to him first. We try to use our influence to make sure the matter does not have to wait too long.'

'With a sharpened spoon?'

'As you say. With a sharpened spoon. Campbell had a quicker death than his victim endured, and she was only nine years old. The life sentence her family must serve will be a little easier because of our efforts.'

'A novel idea for a victim support group.'

'I'm glad you think so. Much more practical than well-meaning psychotherapists, don't you agree?'

'One point. You said Colin had not named your contact with the families. Why?'

'Perhaps because you did manage to resurrect the file your husband had buried so carefully. I assume he did not want to risk you finding out and wrecking his careful research with an accidental comment at the wrong moment, and in the wrong place.'

'Was that why he didn't tell me?'

'It is a reasonable assumption, after all, you work with

107

the man. He is a good friend of yours, and you might have let something slip.'

There was no need for Sue to ask directions to the house of the friend, she knew it well. It was part of a Victorian terrace in Streatham Park, quiet, respectable, close to a church.

Sue sat in the car looking at the home at the end of steps and a small garden. Behind the ground-floor curtains there was a light. She closed her eyes and pictured the room as she had last seen it. Then, she had sat with Colin after a good meal. They had drunk coffee and fine whisky listening to a born raconteur enlivening the evening with unprintable gossip.

Her steps to the front door were slow, her finger on the button reluctant until a whiplash of anger at the deceit made her press it again, firmly this time.

Sue was ushered into friendly warmth, winter flowers in a bowl on the table marking the passage of the seasons. Last time it had been late roses.

Left alone with her host she looked at him with a mixture of fury, despair, exhaustion. 'Watty, why?'

'You met them, Sue. Some of them told me, the ones you visited. How many did you go and see? Three families? Do you have any idea how many I've spent my time with over the years? Do you wonder I hate the bastards who cause such misery?' The kindly face was twisted by remembered torment. 'I can't go to the prisons and drag 'em out by the scruff of the neck, but I can do the next best thing.'

'Make sure they die?'

'Why not?'

Watty's wife, Joyce, had left them alone in the warm sitting room. The Christmas tree in the corner had presents underneath, ready for the next day. The couch and chairs were a little worn, but comfortable. The smell of tobacco from Watty's pipe gave an illusion of the countryside, enhanced by gas flames curling round log shapes on the hearth.

Sue sighed. 'How did it begin?'

'I couldn't tell you, not exactly. I went straight for news work as soon as I left school. Whichever paper I was on I trailed the crime man round Glasgow. Early on I saw some pretty gruesome sights. I found I could handle those, it was the people I had difficulty with. Learning to get copy while trying to be sympathetic – God, it was hard. Decent, careful folk, their lives turned upside down by some maniac . . .'

Watty leaned forward, his elbows on his knees as he gazed at the patterned swirls of brown in the fawn carpet.

'They laughed at me, the boys in the newsroom. I'd go back afterwards, when the trial was over, to see how the poor sods were coping. Gradually, it began to crystallize. I suppose it was the wee Drummond girl. You'll no remember, it was way before your time. The man that did for her was in Barlinnie. He choked on his own porridge. It happens if someone fills your mouth too full and then doesna let you get your breath. A real hoo-ha it caused. I went back to the Drummonds. The mother was sitting greeting. "Thank God," she kept saying, in between wiping away at her tears.'

'So that made you decide to take the law into your own hands?'

'No way. I stuck wi' the law, all the way. I still do.' He smiled at her look of disbelief. 'All we've ever done is let things happen.'

'But you had no right –'

'No? The first step was always taken by the person who chose to murder. Their decision to kill set the ball rolling. Once all the legal formalities were gone through, then we met and talked about the families left to suffer for what he had done.'

'I still say hanging's not the answer for murder.'

'Aye lass, and you're right. Why should a husband

who's throttled a cheating bitch of a wife swing for her, or a son who helps his dying mother out of pain. Then there's a father who's been raping his daughters until his wife sticks a breadknife in him. She needs a medal, not executing.'

A little mollified, Sue leaned back against the comfort of her chair. Watty could see her pallor, the purple bruising of exhaustion under her eyes. He shook his head, his mouth a grim line.

'Then there's a man who cold-bloodedly slaughters children. He's different, and in my book he's forfeited the right to live. When hanging stopped, men like that were put away and were expected to do time which stretched beyond most people's imaginations. The day came when they started coming out, men who would normally have been sludge in the quicklime after they'd been hanged. The killings started again. My father predicted it. He was in the police, in Glasgow. I'm just glad he didn't live to see what's happened. These last years, it's gone badly wrong. All society cares about's the criminal.'

'That's not strictly true.'

'Isn't it? Rules of evidence, taped and videoed statements? Weekend leave for psychopaths? There's a huge army of do-gooders helping the little sods. Suppose one rapes a virgin? Well, as long as you see she gets a good holiday afterwards, what's it matter? Let's spend a small fortune rehabilitating the hell-hound, let him know how much we all care about him, after all he had a terrible childhood, his mammy never smacking him.'

Watty's voice was rising with his anger. He rose and began to pace the small room.

'Perhaps he kills prostitutes instead,' Watty went on. 'So what? Our colleagues of the gutter press will be after his relatives to pay them for their stories – the same relatives who made him a murderer.'

Watty looked down at Sue, the agony on his features illumined by a fierce light.

'Think of our own pages,' he went on. 'Article after

article on the breakup of families. Then look at the crime reports. Day after day it's a wife picked out by a maniac to be butchered, a child. Why are they chosen? How often is it because they come from good homes, caring homes, from real families? We can't have that, can we? We can't have happy families. It makes our poor little criminals feel so disadvantaged, so it's only reasonable they abuse a child to death, then that family can be wrecked, just like all the others.'

Watty went to the fireplace, leaning on the mantel while he gazed into the flames, seeing in them the hell of his experiences. He turned to Sue.

'Rogue animals are expelled from the herd, or killed by their own. Come on, lass. You're the scientist. You know that's true. What about the Tamils? When the cry goes up "Amok", it's the duty of everyone to see the madman dies. All our group's done is let nature take its course, unhindered by do-gooders.'

Watty threw himself into his chair, reaching into his pocket for his pipe. He filled it, tamped it down, lit it. The movements and the nicotine coursing through his bloodstream calmed him.

'Do-gooders,' he snorted, smoke trickling from his nostrils. 'They've started attacking the families of those wee souls tortured and butchered, then hidden on the Yorkshire moors.' He arranged his features into a prissy expression, the mouth a small 'o'. '"Poor dear Myra is a good girl now. You must forgive her and forget all the evil things she's done to you and yours. It's wrong for you to go on hating her." What do they know? Have they sat with a mother who's lost a child that way? You can bet they've been too busy chasing after the criminal to smother them in sympathy, there's been no time to spare for the bereaved.'

'You believe that for some crimes there is no forgiveness?'

'Not this side of heaven.' He was very sure. 'You understand that now, don't you?'

'Because of Colin?' she asked him.

'Yes.'

Sue lay in her chair drained of thought, emotion, and the room was still. 'So why did he have to die?'

'I don't know, lass. I wish to God I did.' There was no doubting the strength of Watty's feelings.

'How did he find out about you?'

'A whisper from one of his clients. Something he noticed in the office, maybe.'

'Bill Farnham was one of you. Colin had him listed.'

'Aye. Colin was a quiet man, but sharp, gey sharp. Martin got us all together to meet Colin, so he could listen to our point of view. Bless the lad, he did too. Listen, I mean.'

'Could one of you have decided he knew too much?'

'Good God, no! It was months ago he pieced it all together. Nobody knew better than that husband of yours there was no way we could be prosecuted, with no hard evidence to take to court. As far as I knew, he'd let go of it.'

'Something was concerning him just before he died. I thought it was one of his cases. Then I guessed it must be to do with this.'

'He might have been on to something else, nothing to do with us. Perhaps the friends of one of his clients thought him dangerous.'

'So you do think he was killed deliberately.'

Watty nodded, looking a little embarrassed.

'Of course! It was you who heard the tapes from the phone tap.'

'I'm sorry, but we had to know. I was the only one who listened to the tapes, and when it was clear you knew nothing, I destroyed them. Your disks are still OK if you want them back.'

She shivered, shaking her head violently. 'No – thank you.'

Watty went to the door, calling as he opened it. 'Joyce, any chance of a cuppa?'

They sat in silence until Joyce carried in a tray. 'I hope you don't mind tea?' she asked Sue. 'When you're married to a Scotsman, that's all he'll drink at home – that or whisky.'

The tea was poured and Joyce went as quickly as she had come, sensing the tension in the atmosphere.

'Drink it up, it'll help,' Watty advised and Sue sipped obediently.

The tendrils of warmth unlocked tight control. 'I thought when I'd worked through Colin's first list I'd know who killed him, but it was a dead end,' she said at last. 'Then tonight I came across the file which started with Lawrence. I really believed he was sure to give me the answer, but all I got was stalemate. It's hopeless, like peeling skins off an onion.'

Sue leaned forward, suddenly earnest. 'I've got to know why he died – I just can't rest till I do. You understand that, don't you, Watty?'

He put down his cup and saucer and moved swiftly to crouch in front of her, holding her hands to warm them with his strength. 'You've no clue?' The voice was anxious, sincere.

Sue looked hard at Watty, seeing only the man she had known since starting at the *Journal*. He had always been kind to her, cheering her with his concern, helping with his advice and odd snippets of information that came his way. Reluctantly she admitted to herself he had even done his damnedest to protect her from the worst of Lawrence's inquiries. Watty deserved the truth.

'A photo. Taken from the video at the station.' She withdrew her hands from his grasp and he stood as Sue reached into her bag for the print. 'If anyone pushed Colin – it was him.'

Watty frowned over the grainy likeness.

'Do you know him?' she asked.

He shook his head. 'And yet I've a feeling I've seen him with someone. Can I have this?'

'It's the only one I have. I can get another copy, if you really want one.'

'Please. You never know,' he smiled at Sue with tired eyes, 'I may have the odd contact who could turn him up.'

'Thanks. I just don't know where to look any more.' She sank against cushions, letting tiredness have its way.

'Are you managing, lass?'

'I think so. Work keeps me busy – it's a godsend. Then I've had my pilgrimages.'

Watty frowned a question and Sue talked of Gerry and the list of victims. When she was ready to leave, Watty excused himself for a moment, returning with a large, brown envelope.

'Thank you.' Sue held it to her, the wallet inside bulky.

'I'm so sorry, lass, but we just had to know.'

Mrs Lavin chided gently. 'Darling, you look worn out.'

'Don't fuss the girl, Daphne. She needs a hot bath and her bed.'

Sue nodded, grateful for the understanding.

'I don't suppose you've had anything to eat?' her mother decided. 'Have your bath, and by the time you get back down there'll be a tray ready for you.'

Her feet were lumps of lead as she struggled to lift them up each stair. By the time she had run her bath and lay soaking Sue only had enough energy to watch droplets of condensation chase each other down the tiles.

Her father's voice roused her. Obediently she rose from the cradling water and dressed in pyjamas and dressing gown as quickly as she could. The bath had soothed, unravelling creases from her mind.

An omelette steamed gently as Sue sat by the fire, cocooned in warmth. She was so sleepy that transferring food into her mouth was carried out in slow motion. Her parents chatted of small affairs, not bothering her with questions, attention. The hum of their voices was soothing, and the omelette was washed down with a cup of hot chocolate.

Other Christmas Eves were in the memory of the three who sat so companionably. Sue with Colin, their love adding to the sense of closeness for them all. Her parents saw again Sue as a child, determined to wait up for Santa Claus. This was not such a night, and gratefully, she crawled into bed.

When she woke it was in the stillness of the early hours. Rain spattered her window, reminding her of unpleasantness outside. Christmas Day. She had been in the same bed last year, Colin beside her. Sue looked at the lighter square of the window in the dark wall of stone.

'Colin?' she whispered, feeling him near.

Sue closed her eyes. There was a certainty in her now. Colin's murderer would be found, and the reason for his death. She was no longer alone in her quest, a growing band of friends working with her. Pippa and Ken, Stephen Childs, Watty – even Martin Lawrence.

'Like peeling skins off an onion,' she had told Watty. Two had come away, and still she had not found her answers. Colin had been preoccupied in the days before his death. She lay in her warm bed and thought of him. The memories had been too poignant for her to bring back before, but in the silence of the Christmas morning, she relived the last days. There had been laughter and love, as well as haste, hard work. Colin had files, frowning as he read through them, while Sue worked at her computer or cooked, washed up, got ready for bed.

Mentally floating, Sue's memory recalled Colin's face in those days, watching his expressions change. He had been hiding something from her. She knew now he did so to protect her, but from what? The question whirled in her mind, faces advancing, retreating, then Colin smiled at her, and she slept.

Christmas Day was endured and passed with few difficulties. After church Mrs Stroat had tried to be charming and failed miserably. Fortunately, her husband's smile achieved all she could not, but friends from Sue's schooldays were awkward, not knowing what to say. Mr Lavin came to the rescue and after fielding his wife from an earnest chat, he drove them home.

Turkey, television, cups of tea and festive cake filled in the remaining hours. The first Christmas without Colin had gone, another milestone passed in the lonely journey.

Next morning Sue needed the crisp challenge of cold air. She took herself for a walk across the common, heading for a copse through which ran a stream. A trickle in summer, now it was in spate, the sound busy. Mrs Willoughby's Hector came bounding up and grunted a welcome. He was followed by his mistress, warmly wrapped against the cold. She looked keenly at Sue, then nodded a silent approval.

'Stick it out, my girl,' Sue was told. 'There'll be hard days ahead still, but you're coping.' The words were bracing, cathartic. 'You're made of the right stuff,' Mrs Willoughby added.

Hector was dragged away from the aromas embedded in a tussock of grass, and through a mist of tears Sue found it suddenly difficult to see the sturdy figure marching on in body-warmer and wellingtons. Mrs Willoughby tugged a tweed hat more firmly in place, and was gone.

Just after New Year Stephen Childs arrived in Islington. He summoned Ken and Pippa and began a council of war.

'The cases Colin had been working on when he was killed, have you got the files?' Stephen asked Ken.

'Thought that's what you'd want,' Ken grinned, handing over sheets of paper clipped together.

Stephen read quickly. 'Can I keep this?'

'Of course,' Ken agreed.

'May I have a copy?' Sue said, her chin jutting, firm.

Stephen and Ken exchanged glances, Stephen nodding

almost imperceptibly. 'Have mine,' said Ken. 'I've another in the office.'

Sue looked through the list of contested cases. Two concerned burglaries, the defendant in each case well known to the police and willing to plead guilty to lessen sentencing. One case involved carrying an offensive weapon, she read. The man was in his fifties and afraid of his neighbour's teenage son. It sounded ridiculous until Sue learned why. The youth's pitbull terrier had been beaten until it was savage. There were witnessed threats of the dog being released on to a tiny grandson of the accused, the threats being taken seriously. Colin had recorded his hopes of an acquittal for the grandfather.

'I don't see much to help us, do you?' she asked Stephen.

'On the face of it, no.'

'Those who had enough sense to plead guilty, they'd have no reason for wanting Colin out of the way,' Ken said quietly. 'He was damned good at seeing they got a reasonable sentence, and the chance of help, if that's what they needed.'

'You wouldn't say he qualified as a do-gooder?' Sue asked.

'God, no!' Ken laughed. 'Colin was as tough as they come with his clients. If they'd earned a stretch, he'd tell them so, and go for mitigation. If there was doubt, then he'd fight.' He pointed to the sheets Sue held. 'That lot knew the score, that's why they wanted him in their corner.'

'What about relatives?' Pippa wanted to know. 'Irate mums and girlfriends screaming "'E wos framed, Guv."'

Ken smiled at Pippa, and Sue had a moment's envy. 'You girls watch too much television.'

'It's how we bring a little excitement into our lives,' Pippa declared archly.

'I should think Sue has enough of that with her job,' Stephen added. 'Her boss is a right pain in the backside.'

'Yesterday's front page?' she queried with a grin.

Stephen nodded. 'The crime wave is solely due to inefficient policing. We're all paid too much, have too much time away from the job on imaginary nervous breakdowns – what else?'

'Too much time shacking up with wives of criminals, not to mention preferring to spend hours playing with typewriters or traffic tickets, instead of facing up to the nasties,' Sue quoted. 'Jepson does love having a pop at you.'

'Why?'

Sue remembered a write-up of the birth of triplets to a PC in Tottenham, a man with three older children. 'What's different about the police?' Jepson had demanded of her. 'Try getting research done into their sperm counts.' Cause and effect again. 'He really is a nutter,' she assured Stephen.

'But he pays you well,' Pippa laughed.

'More important,' Sue argued, 'he mostly lets me do my job as I want to.'

'Does he respect scientists, or does he fear them, I wonder,' Stephen mused.

'It's not scientists he's running scared of at the moment,' she laughed, thinking of Jepson's attempts at late fatherhood.

'Should I know what he wanted?' Bobby Chalmers, waiting outside Jepson's office, was almost panting in his eagerness.

'No.' Sue walked on.

'If it was to do with the campaign, then surely I should be told, too.'

'He's asked me to do an interview,' she explained patiently.

'Who with?'

'Until I've made some phone calls, I won't know myself.'

'Is it related to the phenols?'

'Heaven alone knows. When I've got my copy ready,

Jepson wants first sight.' Sue saw a gleam come into the blue eyes, a plan beginning to shape. It would be in Bobby's nature to read her work and get the idea to Jepson first, claiming any possible credit. 'He said first sight, and if anyone beats him to it, he'll have their guts for garters. You know that by now, surely.'

Bobby flushed and rushed into the men's toilets, bumping into Watty.

'What's got into him?' he demanded.

Sue explained.

'So, the latest bimbette is still without child, I suspect,' he grinned.

'I never even said who I'm to interview.'

'You don't have to. My money's on the leading expert on male infertility. Ideally, it's for an article to help all the poor little men who've over-indulged on your blasted chemicals. In reality, Jepson's decided to go and get himself seen to.'

'How about a vet?'

'You're getting as bad as me,' Watty laughed, and put an arm around Sue's shoulders as they headed back to work. 'Any news about Woolly-hat?'

'Nothing. He seems completely anonymous. Stephen Childs is working on it, unofficially.'

'I've met him. He's damned good, not like the fly-boys who come out with gleaming teeth when the press arrives. Has he no idea?'

'I'm not sure,' Sue said slowly. 'I get the feeling he has a glimmer.'

'Well lass, he won't tell you until he's certain.'

'No help from your contacts?'

'Not so far. The photo makes it hard to see the features clearly, and that hat covers too many clues. Still, I'll keep on asking around.'

'Thanks, Watty.'

Two days later Sue had to visit a publisher of scientific

textbooks and went into work later than usual. Instead of the purposeful hum which normally greeted her, there was a sense of uncertainty, of suppressed excitement. Cary Mitchell, the gossip columnist, hurried past, his Savile Row tailoring immaculate, but his blue silk tie had come adrift and was flying over his shoulder. Just behind him were two satellites, young ladies on duty from their Sloane Square homes. Kate followed, her hair an aureole of fire around the glee of her expression.

'What's happened?' Sue asked.

'Haven't you heard? Dear old Jepson, he insisted on trying everything.'

'Kate, spell it out.'

'He was being just a trifle kinky with his latest. Not a good idea at his age, but he was very sensitive on that subject.'

'And?'

'Stroke, darling. He's prostrate in the Royal Free, Mrs Jepson in attendance. God knows what happened to the tart. I expect she was hurried away.'

'What will happen here?'

'It already has. Sam's taken over. Teensy Bobby's collaboration with Maginty's has been axed, and the little horror shunted over to that pseudo-science mag the Jepson group owns. The one with the gory pictures.'

'*Science For Tomorrow*?'

'That's the one. Ghastly prose style – they deserve the little beast.'

Sue sat at her console and checked her mail. There was a general memo from Sam, which had gone to everyone, stating only the facts of the change in editorial control. Other matters were internal, requests for data dealt with quickly, copy written up and checked by Beth. Only as she tidied her desk, ready to leave for lunch, did Sue find the note.

'Have a lead,' Watty had written. 'Fingers crossed, lass.'

120

Chapter Seven

The next hours were hectic, the offices of the *Journal* abuzz with gossip, rumour, fear. Getting in and out of the main doors proved difficult, the rest of Wapping determined to get headlines and copy from the imagery of the autocratic Jepson nearly dead in his girlfriend's bed. It was whispered that the ambulance men who kept Jepson alive did so with wide grins on their faces, the equipment he had felt necessary to get his spermatozoa moving usually found in the sleazier parts of Soho.

'Where's Watty?' Sue had asked.

'Missing all the fun,' Jonah, Watty's second-in-command, replied. 'He's chasing up a whisper he had yesterday.'

'Haven't you heard from him at all?'

'Nope. Don't expect to. He phoned in about four to check there was nothing big on. I'm doing the Bailey anyway. Keith's at Lewes for the sentencing there, and we've stringers doing the rest. Quiet time for us, for a change.'

'Let me know if he calls in again. I need to talk to him.'

Jonah looked up at Sue, eyes sharp in lined skin, his bald head gleaming in the pseudo-daylight from the ceiling. 'Can I help?'

'No – thanks, though. It's something personal.'

'Well, any time. I owe you one for explaining what the scene-of-crime boys were after in that flat in Hans Crescent. The marvels of modern science!'

Sue sighed. 'You'd think the villains would realize that

no matter where they go or what they do they leave traces and can be caught.'

Jonah laughed, then broke off, coughing, wheezing, his lungs betraying him. 'Don't you believe it,' he said when he could speak again. 'If you're born twisted, that's the way you'll go. I've sat through trials listening to the time and patience – yes, and intelligence, used to commit crime after crime. It's unbelievable. Half the effort in the straight world would have seen the morons millionaires, but no, it's got to be done crooked or it's not kosher.'

'Like some enormous game.'

'You're right. I suspect it's as old as the hills. Probably little cave-boys played cops and robbers.'

'Imitating the grown ups?'

'Of course. Can't you just see it? A whole family working hard to gather seeds and nuts for the winter. Along comes a lazy bastard in lion's skin, bops them with a mammoth's thigh bone and steals the lot. There's nothing new in what we do.'

'Not even for me?' Sue laughed.

'Science? How do you think Mrs Cave Man knew which seeds to grow? What plants to use for medicine? Real science that was. She couldn't go to a nice shiny university like you dolly birds.' His grin shone in pale blue eyes, moved aside deep lines.

'You put me to shame, Jonah. I'd better get a lion's skin ordered and get hunting.'

'Wait till it's summer, Sue. Much more fun.'

Sue laughed and walked away, her spirits lifted by the banter. Fun. Would there ever be room in her life for that again? It needed an untroubled mind, free of black holes absorbing all energy.

'Sue! Have you heard?' Kate advanced, eyes gleaming with unholy satisfaction.

'Something new?'

'Cary.'

'What's he done?' Sue asked.

'Nothing. His budget's been slashed,' Kate said with relish.

'Why? His page is worth it to the paper.' Cary Mitchell's gossip items led with the news of the rich and famous.

'Not space, darling. Cary's still got to turn in the proverbial, but he can't have so many luvvies trailing him all day. Apparently Sam told him bluntly the *Journal* was in the business of daily news, not subsidizing delinquent aristocracy. If Cary wanted that, he must go and be a publisher of coffee-table glossies, like some we could mention.'

'He must be livid.'

'Sam or Cary? Sam's always been against keeping little duckies happy so Cary can get himself invited to the odd ball or box at the races.'

'Sam's got a point. If Cary's as good as he believes he is, he'd get the invites anyway.'

'Of course! But how else can he keep a fleet of bimbos and not have his wife divorce him? Remember she's the one with the lolly.'

'Poor Cary.'

'Poor Cary my –'

Sue was spared more as Beth appeared.

'Got a minute?' Beth asked Sue. 'Check this for me.' She handed Sue tomorrow's article set out with headline, photos, captions.

'I don't usually need to.'

'Sam's overseeing the presentations.'

'I see what you mean,' Sue agreed, reading quickly and handing back the sheet with a nod of approval. With Sam Haddleston in mind Sue sorted her desk, mail, files, working with the sense of purpose which had invaded the whole office. The *Journal* was at last under the control of a man who knew the business inside out. He was no rich man playing with a toy, but a tough professional who would use the interregnum to prove he could do the top job. The board would pass him by at their peril. Meanwhile, the staff would be careful.

Gerry phoned from Whitechapel with the news of a medical breakthrough doing the rounds of the hospitals. It took much telephoning and persuading, but finally Sue had eight hundred words and explanatory diagrams. She thanked God for the computer program that made the drawings and labellings so easy for her. Beth took over and Sam approved, pleased the *Journal* had a scoop on the academic side.

'Makes a change from all that sex we've been peddling recently,' he told Sue. 'Jepson's obsession with it only got him a bed in hospital.'

'There are a lot of men terrified by their sperm count,' she had answered demurely.

'But I'm not one of them,' he insisted.

Sue watched him swivel in the great black chair. Fair, compact, he was the antithesis of Jepson. Sam's cuffs were not held orderly with masses of silver, his sleeves were rolled high above his elbows. The knot of his tie was loosened, but it would take only seconds for him to tighten it and don the suit jacket a hand's reach away.

'You did the research behind that campaign we've been running?' he asked.

'The nonyl phenols? Yes.'

'I read your memos. Some of the plastics people are still using the stuff. Sheep-dip. Still phenols?'

'These days most are organo-phosphate based. They sound safe, but there are claims they can act like nerve gases on farmers using them.'

The black chair was swivelled. 'The campaign you've been running has to stop, at least in its present form, but we can't expose just how useless it was.'

Sue understood. Jepson was influential as well as rich. He might be in a sick bed, but his friends and allies in the money markets would be watching events at the paper. If Sam appeared to belittle Jepson in any way, the financial rug would be pulled out from under the *Journal*.

She smiled reassuringly. 'It hasn't been a complete waste. The public are more aware of the dangers, and that's no bad thing. Let's face it, if the government's already agreed to ban the use of nonyl phenols within the next ten years, no matter how useful they are to industry, there's a compelling reason. It hasn't even needed media involvement to get politicians that far.'

'They must be running scared for their own skins.'

'What is frightening is that in spite of all that, some producers will go on using them well into the future – unless they're stopped.'

Sam frowned. 'Bastards like that need rooting out.' He paused, marshalling his thoughts. 'I'll give you young Anil Naib to replace the boy we sent to the mag. What's-his-name.'

'Bobby Chalmers.'

'That's the lad. We've cut out Maginty's and we'll go for in-depth investigations instead. Anil can do the footwork, he's as good as a ferret any day. It'll be up to you to go on explaining the dangers to the public.'

'Instead of worrying them about their sperm count, we scare them witless about the nerve gas effect?'

His face was bland, his eyes ready to smile. 'Which would concern you?' he said as Cary Mitchell barged into the room, giving Sue a chance to escape.

It was with a sigh of relief that she left for home. The drizzle which met her was almost refreshing, its coldness making her hurry to the car. With wipers swishing, head-lights reflecting from drenched figures hurrying on pave-ments, cars and trucks with steaming exhausts, Sue felt isolated in a capsule, her tiredness making her drowsy.

The flat welcomed her. Wet clothes shed, Sue began to run hot water into the bath before going to the answer-phone. There was one call from Pippa, saying she was going out with Ken. There would be no cosy chat in front of the fire tonight. Sue looked at the couch, longing to see Colin sprawled there, but the cushions were plump, smooth. She sighed, sad she could bear to go for her bath with only a prickling at the back of her eyes. Time was working, dragging Colin's shadow away.

'Come on,' Sue told herself, forcing tired legs to walk to the bathroom.

A long hot soak later she was ready to forage in the fridge before settling in front of the fire with tomorrow's *Journal*. Sue read it carefully, looking for the changes Sam Haddleston had made in the format of the pages. At first glance there was little apparent difference, the common appeal as it always had been. As she read on, Sue realized a shift in the importance of syntax. Articles had a greater crispness, impact. The subs must have been hard at it, Sue decided, smiling to herself. The compositors had really extended themselves as well. She was hard pressed to find any spelling mistakes at all. The new broom was certainly sweeping clean.

In bed and ready for sleep, Sue's mind drifted towards the *Journal's* unseen compositors. They were an endangered species, if the rumours about new systems were true. Reporters typing their copy straight on to the presses? It would save time, cash, cock-ups. Yet how could people like Paula learn their trade without subs to guide and compositors to present? Sue smiled faintly in the darkness. She knew too many reporters who had trouble spelling properly.

Her mind wandered around the missing spelling mistakes. Sam Haddleston had a bee in his bonnet about accuracy. Perhaps it was his North Yorkshire school ethic breaking through. Dreamily, shadows of old pages haunted her, dappled Canadian sunlight drifting through the Avonlea stories. They had been written a world away and part of Sue's childhood fantasy lands, yet there had always been a spelling bee in the offing. Accuracy was important. She had certainly needed it for her science studies. Make a spelling mistake in Zoology and you could have the wrong muscle, even the wrong animal. Her thoughts wandered. In chemistry it could mean a different compound, not funny if the chemical was a medicine. As for physics, a mistake in that field could set off the wrong bomb.

126

Sighing, Sue wriggled herself comfortable. Tomorrow she might go and see Sam to suggest he run a spelling project, prizes for the best spellers amongst the young. She pictured him beset by anxious mums, each determined their child be the winner. A chuckle escaped her, silenced as she slept.

Next morning, in the quiet time before London is fully awake, Sue hurried through her morning chores. For once she felt like cooking herself some breakfast, and was busily stirring beaten eggs as they set when the phone rang. With the pan in one hand, Sue responded to the demand, hoping it would be a short call.

'Sue? Stephen Childs. I was checking reports just in. Your friend, Watson Skinner. Was he the one you wanted the spare photograph for?'

'What's wrong?'

'His wife's reported him missing.'

Streatham seemed an eternity away, the early morning traffic a jungle. At last Sue drew up outside the quiet house and sat for a moment, gathering her breath and her courage as she remembered her last visit.

Joyce opened the door, hope dying as she saw Sue. 'You'd better come in.'

'There's no news?'

Helen, Watty's younger daughter, came from the kitchen. Her face was a mask, emotions put on one side for her mother's sake. 'Tea?'

Joyce sipped at what must have been the umpteenth cup offered to her in the last hours. 'The people who work with him have been so kind.' Joyce was a pretty woman in spite of the strain. Her red hair was lighter than it had been, but her years still sat easily. 'That young reporter, Keith, stayed in the office all night waiting for a message. Jonah was here with us until six, this morning. He hasn't a clue what Watson was after.'

'Did Watty record the call from his informant?' Sue wanted to know.

Joyce was puzzled. 'Why should he?'

'Odd messages usually are. Would you mind if I called the office?'

Sue went out into the hall, leaving mother and daughter silent, the heat of their cups thawing cold fingers.

'Jonah, I'm at Watty's. Anything?'

'Nothing. I've tried ringing round a few hopefuls, but it's no go.'

'Listen, the phone call Watty got, did he tape it?'

'Yes, I've played it a dozen times. Nothing to help. The caller only spoke the odd word.'

'Jonah, could you make a copy of the tape, and put it somewhere safe?'

Sue remembered the almost-lost video from the station.

'Are you coming in?' Jonah was wheezing badly.

'I'll see if I can help here. Sam will understand.'

The acting editor not only understood, he was in the house almost before Sue had finished talking. His brisk manner and firm handshake enlivened Joyce and Helen, tired by a night's vigil.

'Glad you're here, Sue,' he said, when Helen went away to make yet another pot of tea and her mother disappeared to freshen up. 'This is a bad business. There's no indication of what he was working on, I checked before I came. One word from an informant and he was off. Jonah thought you might have some idea what lead he was chasing.'

'Me? Why?'

'Something about a photograph?'

Sue froze, feeling the inner tremblings of panic about to erupt. 'Please God, no.'

'Come on. It's my paper. I have to know what's happening.'

Sue explained as briefly as she could. When she finished, Sam stood, restless.

'So Watty went off after some maniac who might have killed your husband?' He punched one hand into the palm of the other. 'What was he thinking of? It's a police matter! There's no way we have the means for chasing crooks. It needs planning, back-up.'

Sam prowled and Sue sensed he was working out his own logistics of the situation. He looked down at her.

'Who was he after?'

'I can't tell you. He seemed to have an idea who might have been behind it, but he wouldn't say. He wanted to be sure. Perhaps he caught up with them.'

'I hope you're wrong,' came with a hiss as Helen carried in a tray of cups and saucers.

Sue thought of Colin, dead and buried, Watty perhaps chasing his killer. 'Not as much as I do.'

There was more tea to drink, more phone calls making Helen run to answer and Joyce sit forward. Her whole body betrayed expectancy before Helen returned, each time shaking her head.

A neighbour arrived, a Mrs Jacobson, older than Joyce and with an air of authority. In a well-cut navy suit and white blouse she was calm, stately, practical, every inch the hospital matron she had been. Joyce and Helen were on their way to their beds before they were aware they were moving.

Mrs Jacobson turned to Sue and Sam, her smile professional behind stylish glasses. 'You must be anxious to get back to work. I'll see to things here, and let you know when Mr Skinner turns up safe and sound.'

Sam was courteous, but adamant the *Journal*'s resources were on call. 'Remember there'll be someone there, day or night, ready to do anything to help,' he insisted.

It was a very small smile he earned from Mrs Jacobson. 'For the moment Mrs Skinner and her daughter need rest. Sleep will be difficult, but at least I can see they're not disturbed. The door bell, phone calls, they're all very upsetting for them just now.' She raised a hand in graceful dismissal, giving Sue and Sam no alternative but to leave.

129

Outside the front gate Sam stopped Sue as she bent to unlock her car door. 'Are you all right?'

'Why shouldn't I be?'

'You've been through something similar, and not so long ago,' he growled.

'You're assuming Watty's dead?'

Sam's eyes were shadowed, his mouth grim. 'It's possible, and you know it.'

'No!' Sue protested. 'He can't be!' She dreaded the truth. 'He mustn't be.'

Sam Haddleston was on his way to the *Journal* offices almost before Sue had time to start her engine. As she threaded through parked cars towards Mitcham Lane, Sue almost envied Sam the luxury of his chauffeur-driven state, but it was not the social emblem enjoyed by Jepson. Sam's car was an office on wheels, and orders would have gone thick and fast to the *Journal* before Bob, his driver, achieved top gear.

When Sue arrived in the vast open space of the office, concern was almost tangible.

'Where's Watty got to?' Kate demanded, tossing her cigarette into a plastic mug of cold coffee on the desk behind Sue's chair. She lit another cigarette. 'We're used to him going off and pretending he's a reincarnated Sherlock, but he's not been gone this long before.'

'There's been no message here at all?'

'Apparently not. God knows where he is. He could be on a jet heading for Bangkok, chasing bloody smugglers for all we know. It would be just like him.'

Jonah was about to walk past, the droop of his jowls echoing his spirits.

'Has anyone checked the airports?' Kate asked him.

'The police and Sam, both. Watty's just vanished.'

Work went on, news was discussed, written about, shaped to size for the compositors. At the next desk to Sue, Anil slammed down his phone, the light of excitement an aura.

'A factory in Bedfordshire. One of the worker's wives is furious her husband's at risk.'

Sue smiled briefly 'Accuracy, Anil. You're implying this worker is a bigamist or a Mormon. Is he?'

'Sue! Don't be so pedantic! You sound just like Beth.'

'Thanks. I'll take it as a compliment. Now, what's up?'

'The man works in a plastics factory. He's been very poorly for months, and the doc says it's his job. He could have inhaled gases which have damn near paralysed him. The wife's heard him talking with his buddies, and they say the stuff they make is due to be banned – but the boss is going to go on producing it and ship it out of the country.'

'What stuff?'

'She didn't say.'

'Have you a number for her?'

Anil looked crestfallen, his thick dark hair slanting across his face like that of a small boy ready to cry.

'Then you'd better get on your way, and take a cameraman with you. Talk to them, the boss, and the doctor. If you can, leave the worker's name out of it. We don't want to be accused of getting him the sack. It comes expensive.'

'Thanks, Sue.'

'Better see if Pete Tym's free. He'd be your best bet.'

'Because he's good with a camera, or because he's big?'

Sue thought of the missing Watty 'Both. Remember you're dealing with people ready to edge past legal methods. They won't like reporters snooping round.'

Anil hurried away and she envied him the hunt for facts. Beth was a good antidote to worry, making Sue concentrate on the work in hand. The day passed in a blur of phone calls as she argued and persuaded, before writing. By evening articles were ready and in the presses, the next day's work roughed out. Kate strode over, slinging a camel wool cape around her.

'Come on. We need a drink.'

'I'll just ring Joyce first.'

Sue did so, ashamed to hear the disappointment in the woman's voice when she realized it was not her husband. There was no news, except that Fiona, the elder daughter, had arrived from Coventry where she was a lecturer. Sue was thoughtful as she pulled on her thick navy coat and hurried after Kate.

The pub along the road was full of journalists. It was the hour of relaxation, servicing a need to unwind before going home to loved ones, or perhaps to theatres, meals, the oblivion of alcohol, whatever appealed.

Not since losing Colin had Sue joined in the evening ritual. It was as though she had never been absent. The familiar reek of cigarette smoke overlaid the sharp tang of hops, whisky, gin. She thought of the long drive home she must make and agreed to a spritzer.

'You're washed out, you need a decent drink,' Kate insisted, adding a double brandy to the list.

'You'll have to sink that,' Sue insisted, 'I'm driving.'

'Do what I do and get a cab,' Kate suggested, covertly examining a newcomer, his tie loosened, his suit expensive.

Sue sipped, bubbles refreshing her palate. As a thirsty group from the *Journal* pushed towards the bar, the man Kate was watching moved closer. Kate manoeuvred herself near enough to be bumped. The man apologized, insisting he find a table for them.

'I'm Kate Jeffries. I write for the *Journal*.'

'I've heard of you – and read you. A hard-hitting lady.'

'Not really,' she cooed, while Sue hid her smile and sipped. 'And you are?'

'Miles Beamish. I'm an accountant, of sorts.'

'For a paper?'

'No.'

It was amusing to watch Kate stalk her prey. Tall, rangy, this one would not be easy, Sue decided. He had the look of someone who had come to terms with divorce and was wary. Kate slid her elbow nearer to him, allowing the musk of her perfume to entice. He leaned back in his chair, out of harm's way Sue had an overwhelming urge to chuckle and hastily bent to get a tissue from her bag.

'What about your friend, does she work with you?'

Sue lifted her head and met grey eyes, their look direct, uncompromising, interested.

'Sue? Yes.' Kate was not too happy the conversation was escaping her. 'Sue Bennett.'

Miles Beamish continued to look at Sue, and she felt warm colour begin to suffuse her skin.

'Do you work for the *Journal*?' he asked.

'She's a science writer,' Kate interrupted, insisting Miles turn his attention away from Sue. She failed.

'Are you, now?' He leaned closer to Sue. 'That's fascinating.'

'Oh, yes. Quite the little blue-stocking, our Sue,' Kate added, a trifle waspishly.

Sue looked at her watch. 'Heavens! I should have been long gone. Sorry, Kate. See you tomorrow.'

Kate's expression softened. Sue had recognized territorial signals and was leaving the field free to her friend. As for Miles Beamish, he smiled enigmatically, bidding Sue farewell with an ironic little salute.

As Sue almost ran to her car her thoughts were still in the warm, dark bar. Kate would have her hooks into the tall stranger by now, she reflected, recognizing a flicker of regret that it should be so.

For Kate it was a game, the social pavanne danced by a man and a woman when they first meet. Sue sat in the car trembling, trying to calm herself, even her breathing. A stranger had been attracted to her and let her know he was willing to take things further. Sue faced the truth. She had felt a response well up. It might have been quickly dashed, but it had been there, and Miles Beamish had seen and understood.

It was too soon, Sue argued silently. Going to the pub had been a mistake, she was not ready to perform normally amongst others. Shakily, her fingers inserted the key in the ignition and she switched on the engine.

Driving soothed her, the need for caution achieving what her will-power had failed to do. The flow of traffic had eased, and ruefully she accepted why so many city workers headed for a bar after work. They could relax, drink, be friendly while commuters headed home. Later, the roads were clear and driving easy.

For once Sue found a parking space very near her front door. Not everything was wrong with her world today. Going up the stairs to her flat she realized what this evening had shown her. She had accepted that one day, perhaps a long way ahead, another man might be part of her life. Was she pushing Colin away? The thought haunted her as she sat late into the night.

A few days later Sue spent the morning at a conservation seminar, meeting old friends. She was able to catch up with news of fieldwork done, and projects in the planning stages. A minor minister spoke at length to the assembly, surprising Sue with a good grasp of his material and a sense of humour. Providing he could survive the next election and stay in his wife's bed at night, he might be someone to watch.

If she had spotted talent, Sue decided, then the predatory females trolling the rich seas of Whitehall would already have him marked as legitimate prey. Was he the man to resist the flattery of an attractive woman intent on replacing his wife? Sue smiled to herself as he gracefully accepted polite applause. Time and the tabloids would tell.

It was not exactly what Darwin had in mind when he argued survival of the fittest, but the ruthless rules of nature still applied. The minister would have to fight off potential parasites if he was going to remain politically healthy.

The buffet was lavish, but vegetarian, and Sue chuckled

as she watched some of the men prowling the tables in search of meat.

The science correspondent of the *Courier* was one. 'Any news of your chap who's gone missing?' he asked.

Sue had very little food in her mouth but it was suddenly impossible to swallow. 'Not yet,' she managed at last.

After lunch she drove to Streatham, putting her arms round a wife who was numb, frozen in time.

Joyce was resigned. 'The girls still hope,' she told Sue. 'If he was alive, I'd know. It's just a feeling I have that he's gone.'

'Could he be somewhere he can't contact you?'

'Locked up, you mean?' Joyce shook her head. 'No.'

When Sue was back in the *Journal* office, Faye called her.

'Mr Haddleston would like to see you as soon as possible.'

'When would be the best time?'

'Now?'

Sue wondered why the summons. Sam was at the desk in the office which had been Jepson's. It no longer looked like a film set. Instead there was a working terminal, orderly piles of paper, files on the central spread of teak.

'You've been to see Joyce Skinner.'

The brusque statement from the man seated behind the desk surprised Sue. 'It was on my way back from the seminar.'

'I'm not accusing you of taking time off – far from it – just glad you went.' Sam glared at Sue as she stood, the angle of her head proud, defiant. 'Sit down, for God's sake, and don't be so touchy.'

Sue did as he asked, but warily.

'I ring every day, but every time I try to talk to Joyce,' Sam went on, 'all I get is someone saying "Not too bad", or "Coping quite well, thank you". How is she? Really?'

'Accepting the fact Watty's dead.'

135

'We're all getting to feel that way.' Sam banged the desk in his frustration. 'I feel responsible!'

'You're not,' Sue protested.

'How can you be so sure?'

She was tempted to tell him of Watty's involvement with Martin Lawrence and Bill Farnham, but it was too risky. Sam was, after all, a good newsman. It would be a story he would find hard not to print. 'I am. It's as simple as that.'

He stared hard at Sue, trying to read her expression. 'OK, I'll take your word for it,' he said at last.

Sue stood, ready to leave.

'Don't go. Tell me about the seminar. Conservation, wasn't it? Anything useful?'

The rumours were true, Sue thought wryly. Sam Haddleston did know everything that happened in the small world of the *Journal*. He waved to her to sit down again and she obeyed.

'There was something,' she said. 'I was talking to a friend just back from the Galapagos.'

Sam frowned, calling on his memory. 'Islands on the equator. Darwin. Ecuador.'

'Government protected as a national park,' Sue added. 'It includes huge areas of sea around the islands where there's not supposed to be heavy commercial fishing.'

'And?'

'Sea cucumbers disappearing by the million, lobsters too.'

'Lobsters I can understand, they feed people, but sea cucumbers? Aren't they some kind of slug?'

Sue laughed. 'To you maybe, but to the night life of Tokyo a delicacy with a high price-tag.'

'Ah! Overfishing for the Asian market.'

'The government have banned the fishermen. The threat to the food chain puts several species of birds in danger of extinction. If that should happen, bang goes a profitable tourist trade.'

'So what's going on?'

'The fishermen see the conservators as their enemies. There have been retaliations.'

Sam nodded, urging Sue to continue.

'The pride and joy of the park is the wide variety of giant turtles. In some remote areas large numbers have been slaughtered, their heads stuck on trees.'

'Tit for tat. You muck us up, we'll have a go at your pets? And the government?'

'They've started air-lifting out threatened colonies of turtles. It's all very hush-hush, but the trouble is that just moving the turtles away from their habitats can prevent them breeding. Either way, they're wiped out – unless politicians can come up with a common-sense solution.'

'That'll be the day!' Sam shook his head. 'What's the worst thing that could happen?'

Sue thought back to the last time she had visited the Galapagos, the volcanic islands hot and dry, dreaming under an endless sun.

'Fire.'

'You're wanted in reception,' Paula called to Sue as she returned to her desk. 'Someone waiting for you.'

Sue ran. It could be news of Watty. A tall figure stood at her approach and Sue halted in front of him, curious as to why he was there.

'Shouldn't it be Kate, not me?' she asked Miles Beamish.

He smiled down at her, grey eyes dancing. 'I like living dangerously.'

'Kate's my friend,' Sue protested.

'She'd be good to have in your corner,' he admitted. 'I'd like to think she's a friend of mine too. There's nothing more on offer for her.'

'Does she know that?' Sue was breathless. It must have been running down the stairs that caused it, she decided.

Miles seemed untroubled by the prospect of Kate's venom. 'The lady's a quick learner, but I'm not here for that. Meet me after you finish work? We could go for a meal.'

Sue had always prided herself on her control. It was strange to be hesitant, a schoolgirl again.

'Please?' Miles persisted.

'I can't. It's too soon . . .'

'I heard about your husband. It was rotten luck.'

Sue looked away and they stood in an awkward silence.

'You have to eat and I know a good Thai restaurant. Come and try it, no strings attached,' he urged.

It would be pleasant to go back into the world of couples, even for one evening. That was all it would be, Sue told herself fiercely. 'Not tonight.' She had promised to go and see Gerry and Richard. 'Thursday?'

Paula was furious. 'That's the third time this week we've slogged our guts out and had everything flung back in our faces.'

Sue wondered yet again how the girl's impetuosity had managed to survive a science degree course. Probably the careers staff of her college had suggested journalism, hoping the fourth estate could absorb the wilful energy.

'The article's not gone for good,' Sue said patiently. 'Scrap the rhetoric and store the data.'

'Doesn't it bother you that something important should be left out of the paper?'

'It's all a question of space,' Sue said calmly. 'Today we're rationed, tomorrow who knows?'

Paula sneered her disgust. 'Sure, today we're rationed, all because some idiot of a cabinet minister can't keep his pants on and grabs the first three pages.'

'That's what I mean. Tomorrow we'll be inundated with calls for information on unwanted pregnancies, the chance of AIDS, statistics on genetic deformities of babies from his age group.'

'I still think it's unfair.'

'Fair? That usually means "What suits me, buster".'

Sue's smile was disarming and Paula was diverted by the offer of coffee. With a mug in each hand, Sue heard her phone trill. Paula picked it up and listened.

'Someone called Childs.'

Sue took the phone, finding it suddenly difficult to breathe. 'Stephen. What is it?'

'A couple of lads were out in Epping Forest. Playing some game they strayed off the main path, kicking up leaves as they went. They found a grave.'

'Is it —'

'There's no positive ID yet, so don't tell anyone, but yes, I think it's Watson Skinner.'

Chapter Eight

Watty had been beaten to death, a shallow grave in a deserted part of the forest his resting place. Sue made her way to the spot as soon as she could. The area swarmed with scene-of-crime officers, blue-and-white tapes marking their efforts. Jonah was with Sam Haddleston, while Sue stood apart, her head bent, grieving for her friend.

'You're shivering. Get in.'

The hand under her elbow was firm as Sam impelled Sue and let go of her only when she sat in the comparative warmth of the car.

'Here.'

A hip flask was open and being thrust at her. 'I don't want –'

'I didn't ask, I'm telling you.'

Jonah heaved himself in beside Sue, wheezing, groggy in the damp air. 'For God's sake drink up, girl, then I can have some,' he advised.

Fire twisted its way into Sue's stomach, bringing alive nerve endings which had minds of their own, each intent on screaming with pain. However much she had railed at Watty for his part in ending the lives of murderers, he did not deserve to lie like a piece of embarrassing garbage, covered with rotting branches.

'It's interesting to see those SOCO boys at work,' Sam said after he had rescued his flask from Jonah's grasp. 'They're not missing a thing.'

'Thought well of Watty, the Bill.' Jonah was morose, grieving. 'He didn't sell 'em short.'

'His father had been a policeman in Glasgow,' Sue added, her throat stiff with the strain of not crying.

'Good God! I never knew that,' Sam was surprised. 'All the years we worked together, he never mentioned it.'

Jonah nodded morosely. 'He never talked about his family unless you dragged it out of him.'

Sue had seen Watty with Joyce, his daughters. His love was intense, private. By talking about them he would have shared out his emotions with others.

The drive back to Wapping was swift, smooth. When Sam walked away to his office and a stream of messages, Sue caught hold of Jonah's sleeve.

'Was there no clue at all where he was going that last day?' she wanted to know.

Jonah sighed. 'I've gone over it again and again. He got the call, tidied up his desk and went.'

'And he said nothing?'

'Not about the call. He did make a crack about Cary Mitchell.'

'Go on,' she urged.

Jonah frowned, struggling to remember. 'Something about him having the intro into all the right places.'

'Why was he interested?'

'I don't know. Kate had just been gossiping on about Cary's parties – some new club he'd been to. Watty perked his ears up and got her to tell him who was running it. Then the call came, he made the crack about Cary, and was off.'

A frisson of excitement went through Sue. 'The club. What was it called.'

'Benjies?' He thought hard, then shook his head. 'No, that's something to do with sandwiches. It was a name like it, or was it the name of the owner?'

Sue held her breath.

'No, it's gone.'

'Jonah, let me know if you remember it. Please.'

*   *   *

Sue almost ran into the office, searching for Cary. A lofty blonde, the last of his entourage, snootily informed her Cary was away for three days at a race meeting in Kentucky. She turned to look for Kate, but Kate was out, lunching with a victim for her column. It was difficult for Sue to contain her impatience. She used the time to get her files organized, trying to persuade Paula to do the same.

'What's the point?' the girl asked, her lower lip demonstrating mutiny.

'If you've got updated files at home and can't get into the office for any reason, you can send copy in.'

'If I'm not here, someone can just fill in for me.'

'Of course they will, and that same someone could get your job.'

'Sacked? Me?'

'This is a daily paper. If you don't produce daily copy, you're not much help to the rest of the staff.'

Paula digested the unfairness of it all. 'You were away three weeks. You kept your job.'

Sue thought back to the wilderness of those interminable days. 'Yes. That's why I have a terminal at home. Maybe you didn't notice I kept on working.'

'You certainly did. I should have had the chance of some of those pieces. How else am I to get experience if you hog it all?'

Sue smiled, but the softness did not reach her eyes. 'If I was out of the way, you wanted to be the one to take my place?'

'Why not?'

'For good?'

Paula realized she was not showing up as well as she would have liked. 'No, of course not,' she said hurriedly.

'But if people are unreliable, they're replaceable?'

'Yes. No.' The girl was irresolute, a new experience for her.

'If I am, so are you.' Sue's chin lifted. 'You wanted more equality with me? Well, it goes all the way.'

It might have been expensively cut trousers Paula wore,

but there was the suggestion of a flounce as she moved away and left Sue in peace.

'I hear you've been looking for me. Sorry, darling, but it was Simpson's food on offer and I wasn't going to hurry that.'

Kate was sleek in her favourite Jean Muir suit, the aroma of rich living emanating from her. Sue grinned, mischief in her eyes.

'I gather it was a lunch that needed a taxi back?'

'Definitely, darling. Now, what part of my vastly superior brain did you want to pick?'

'New clubs.'

'West End?'

'Yes.'

Kate's eyes narrowed as she looked at Sue. 'Are you coming back to a social life?'

'Not me. A cousin of sorts is due over from the States. He likes trying out new eating places.' It was just as well Kate had never met Philip. Middle-aged, respectable, he would run a mile from London's nightlife.

'Does he need help?' Kate began to look interested.

'No, but I do,' Sue told her firmly.

'OK, sweetie. Let's see. There's Georgio's, that's Fulham way. Then there's one in South Molton Street. Baynes. It's pricey but then the food's supposed to be superb. The chef's been pinched from that Georgian manor in Kent.'

'Who's running it?' Sue's question was offhand, as she bent her head to make a note in her diary.

'Denny Culford.'

Sue looked up, frowning a little. 'The name rings a bell.'

'A precious little creep, but very well-connected through Mama. Cary does him occasionally. He was thrown out of that expensive comprehensive near Windsor. I gather he got other snotty-nosed little brats to do his fagging, paying them with cannabis. It didn't go down too well. After that Marlborough had a go for a while, but they refused him the sixth form and nowhere else was willing. It didn't

143

matter, there's plenty of dosh in the family coffers, and Denny likes organizing things.'

'I remember him now. The party boy.'

'The very same. Only the young of the dripping wealthy were ever invited. Eventually their mommas and poppas put a stop to his antics. He was too young to jail for drug dealing, and it was all hushed up. More recently he's been in on the raves.'

'Why a club in Town?'

'He's just working his way up, or down, depending on how you view the idiot rich.'

Kate drifted off to write up her interview. Sue watched her go. Kate might look tiddly but the copy would be immaculately clear and as tough as ever. Lunch at Simpson's did not buy her silence, not even a slurred phrase.

Sue went to find Jonah. He was slowly picking at the keys of his computer, his heavy-lidded eyes hiding his thoughts. She leaned on his terminal.

'Baynes.'

He looked up, private misery retreating. 'So?'

'The new club. Run by Denny Culford.'

'That's the one.' He sat up, rubbing his chin hard as he tried to remember. 'Denny Culford. Front man. Watty thought Culford put up a slice of the cash, but there was someone else in it with him.'

'Not the chef?'

'No way. He's not got that kind of money and no bank's going to lend out on a new boy's cooking skills for a place that expensive. No, Watty guessed there's another player.'

'He didn't say who?'

'Nope.'

It was too early for the evening's first customers at Baynes when Sue left the tube at Bond Street and headed for South Molton Street. Just what she expected to find she had no idea. It was too cold to dawdle and the brisk pace Sue set herself soon brought her to Brook Street, without her being able to identify the club for which she was looking. Deciding to wait a while before retracing her steps, she turned up into the next thoroughfare, fascinated by the name high on the wall. Haunch of Venison Yard. She stood for a moment, picturing life as it must have been when the name had been earned. Cold began to penetrate and, shivering, she hurried on.

A man came quickly from her left. Because of his speed he had not seen Sue, and there was a collision, the man steadying her in the light from the street lamp. Aware of his keen scrutiny she apologized, as did he, his accent incongruous. Only after he was in his car and had driven off did Sue begin to question the accidental meeting. A very solid man, she decided, middle-aged and fit. He must have been well-to-do judging by the silky feel of his thick wool coat against her cheek. The aroma of a good cigar had hung about him, but all she had seen and felt in the brief encounter argued with his strong east London vowels.

Someone who must have made good the hard way, she concluded as she went back along South Molton Street. This time Sue walked more slowly. 'Baynes' was etched on a discreet brass plate set in a wall on her right. On either side of the high black door stood twin bay trees, their dark green balls of leaves trimmed and pampered. There was no sign of anything which might have indicated this was anything other than a high-class business masquerading as someone's home. Disappointed, Sue went back to Islington and the calm of her flat.

'Where have you been?' Pippa's voice was light, cheerful on the phone.

'I had to go into Town for something.'

'Shopping! What fun. Listen, we want you to come with us this evening. Say you will.'

'Oh, Pippa. I don't know.'

'It's nothing heavy, just a gallery do. You'd like the paintings and it would be a change from four walls and me wittering on at you endlessly.'

Sue laughed. 'Witter you don't.'

'Get your glad rags on. We'll call for you in fifteen minutes. Ken says he'll drive, so we can drink.'

'Pale plonk?'

'We can always get a bite to eat afterwards, if the mood takes us.'

'OK,' she said at last, pleasing Pippa. It would be a practice run for Thursday. Sue hunted through her wardrobe for something to wear. Not black, she decided. There had been too much black, and Watty had hated mourning rites.

Watty. He was there with her, his rolling voice with its warm burr roasting her and insisting she got on with her life and enjoyed it. That meant dinner with Miles. Should she cancel Thursday? It might be better to do so rather than disappoint Miles by being an awkward guest. She had become used to being with Colin, it would not be easy with anyone else.

She checked the time and was surprised to see how much had passed since Pippa phoned. She would have to hurry. Resolutely she put aside memories of past evenings, holding up dresses for Colin's scrutiny, waiting for the smile of approval that always began in his eyes.

'This won't do,' she scolded herself out loud. 'Get a move on. You don't want to keep them waiting.'

By now she was used to the extra space in the wardrobe, Colin's clothes long gone to a friend who was a vicar in Lancashire. Backwards and forwards she swished the clothes, unable to make up her mind. A bright colour was not on, she thought, and settled for an old favourite in dark emerald. As she clipped on gold earrings Sue saw that while makeup hid the pallor to which she had become accustomed, there was little she could do to hide the thinness of her body. The habit of getting her hair cut regularly meant that a quick brush had it swinging silkily away from her face.

Stepping back from the mirror Sue took a good look at herself, aware of excitement beginning to build. It felt good to be going out with friends, anticipate a pleasant evening.

The gallery was not too crowded. Voices were not strident, the wine was palatable, the savouries fresh and tasty. One or two of the men she met made it clear they were attracted to her. She was polite, quietly chilling away any further meetings, but secretly pleased they had been suggested. In the midst of a flurry of flashbulbs she caught one of Pippa's smiles to Ken, delighted their scheme for her was working.

Concentrating hard on a portrait of a brooding child Sue accepted that the pace of life was dragging her along with it. Mrs Willoughby came to mind, incongruous in that setting with her tweed hat and body warmer. She was a burst of common-sense against the effete drapery of titled ladies and oozing bosoms of actresses, all anxious for the camera's eye. Sue tired suddenly, yearning for peace, quiet. It was easier to be at home alone, her memories filling the rooms with Colin. She could hear Mrs Willoughby's voice. 'Time to get yourself dragged back in, my dear. Just go with the flow. One day you'll start swimming again.'

The evening with Miles might not have been a good swim, but it was a very pleasant paddle, Sue decided as she unlocked the door of her flat. He had been an excellent companion, sensing her hesitancy and not forcing her to be part of an endless social conversation.

Her first impression of Miles had been an astute one. Divorce had ended an unhappy marriage. It had not only left him wary, it had also robbed him of his son. He missed the boy, longing to hear his voice at the end of each day and be wakened by him each morning.

Sue was a good listener and, as the evening passed and

the aromatic food appeared, she had watched Miles relax and shed some of his world-weariness, becoming younger as he did so.

'Thank you for coming, and being so patient with me. I don't know when I've talked like that. I'm sorry,' he had said simply, 'it must have been boring for you.'

She had enjoyed his company and had promised to see him again.

'I won't talk about James all night, I promise,' Miles had laughed.

As Sue cleaned her teeth, ready for sleep, she thought of him again, understanding what he endured. Bereavement came in many forms.

Since the news of Watty's death, Sam had set an even more cracking pace for his staff. The work helped, the daily rhythm numbing the sense of loss. Although not tall, Watty had been larger than life. His wry Scots wit, his deep-throated chuckle were missed at every turn. Life in the *Journal* offices and corridors seemed very dull and mundane.

The result of the inquest into his death came as no surprise. 'Murder by person, or persons, unknown,' the coroner announced, before offering Joyce his condolences. The burial was quiet, as private as his will decreed. Only Joyce and her daughters were to see him laid to rest.

Watty's friends had a need to grieve and gathered a week later, with his family, in St Bride's, Fleet Street. It was not so much a memorial service as a huddling together for comfort.

Sue was interested to see so many from Colin's list there. Bill Farnham and Martin Lawrence both made a point of talking to her afterwards, the bustle of nearby Fleet Street quieter than it had been when Watty was a regular inhabitant. Her conversations with them were not lost on Sam.

'You've got some unexpected friends,' he remarked as

they stood in the sitting room of the Wattys' house and were fed tea, sandwiches, whisky by Helen and Fiona.

'Me? Not really. Bill Farnham was the senior partner in Colin's firm.'

'And the would-be His Lordship?'

'Martin Lawrence? I met him recently.'

'To do with your husband's accident?'

Sue looked hard at Sam, surprised by the question. 'Yes. Why do you ask?'

'No reason. Just a reporter's instinct, I suppose. Is there a story there?'

She thought of what could not be proved. 'No.'

The finality in her voice appeared to convince him, but Sue guessed the idea had been filed away for future reference. They watched Helen and Fiona deal gently with their mother.

'Watty has two fine girls. He'll live on.' Sam's voice had in it echoes of the loss he felt.

Sue sighed, trying to stifle the sound and her own feelings.

'I'm sorry. That was thoughtless of me.' Sam was contrite.

'Because Colin died too soon for children? It's not your fault. Nor his.'

'You mean –?'

'Oh, no. It's just we decided to wait. We were thinking it was time to start a family then . . .' Tears prickled at the back of her eyes.

'Look, I have to go and see some friends. Come with me.'

'I couldn't.'

'Why not? Their dinner table's the most elastic one I know.'

Sam would brook no further argument, and after saying goodbye to Joyce and her daughters, Sue sat back in the luxury of Sam's car. He drove more swiftly than his chauffeur, weaving expertly in and out of the early evening streams of traffic.

'Where are we going?'

'Not far. Blackheath.'

Their destination was a large terraced house facing Blackheath Vale. Sam held open the car door for Sue.

She swung her legs out, then sat looking up at him. 'You still haven't told me who lives here, nor why you've insisted I come.'

'I told you, friends of mine. Their names are Celia and Peter and they have three young children. Eventually you will be fed extremely well, but first you may have to read stories, play with ducks in a bath, or even peel potatoes. After the kind of day you've had, this is just the place you should be.' He smiled and held out his hand. 'Come on.'

There was a scampering of feet and excited arguing before the door was opened to his ring. With cries of 'Uncle Sammy', he was mounted by three wriggling creatures. Sue gradually identified a boy of about six, and two girls who could have been three and four years old. They were all tow-haired, lively, noisy.

'Let him be, you little horrors,' a deep voice commanded, 'and take him down to the kitchen.'

Instant obedience was the order of the day. The boy dragged Sam along the hall and towards the stairs which led downwards. Two small, warm sets of fingers attached themselves to Sue's cold hands and pulled her in the same direction. The children's father was tall and thin, bending a greying head to Sue as he apologized for his offspring in a voice warm with pride.

For Sue it was a magical time in the huge room which faced a long garden. A small, serene woman moved from sink to stove, stopping to smile at Sue.

'I'm glad you've come. I'm Celia. The one who looks like a fallen choirboy is Adam, and the two young ladies who won't let go of you are Rosalind and Phoebe.' She laughed, an infectious, throaty chuckle. 'Yes, we do sound like the cast of *As You Like It*. I'm afraid we've probably put the children off Shakespeare for life.'

Peter was an excellent host. He amused them with wry

anecdotes as he encouraged them to eat and plied them with wine. Sue quickly lost her shyness, drinking sparingly, while Sam only accepted apple juice. The conversation flowed easily as the food was served and eaten. All of them helped stack the dish-washer and carry coffee, mugs, cream, upstairs to the sitting room. With the door left open a child's cry could be heard, but there was silence from above.

Comfortable chairs welcomed them in the pleasant room, flames licking around logs in the basket of a Victorian fireplace. One wall, banked with books, faced a bay window curtained cheerfully with huge red poppies, and pools of light illumined without strain. Conversation was easy, unforced, and the talk was of plays, books, music.

Although Sue was relaxed and enjoying the company she could feel tiredness dragging at her. Sam saw her increasing pallor and unobtrusively began the thanks and goodbyes.

'Why are you going so soon?' Peter queried.

'I've got to get Sue home. She's got a dreadful boss who'll bawl her out if she's in late tomorrow, or worse, falls asleep on the job,' Sam told him with mock severity.

'They were so nice,' Sue said sleepily, as the car rolled towards Islington. 'Thank you for taking me. It felt like a home where nothing bad ever happens. Such a change from funerals.'

'Oh, they're used to those, I'm afraid,' Sam told her quietly. 'Celia's first husband was in the army. Northern Ireland. A land mine.' The words came with difficulty. 'He was my brother.'

'I'm so sorry,' Sue told him, the words inadequate.

'She took it badly. As far as Celia was concerned her life had ended too. Peter decided otherwise. It took him a long time, but he got what he wanted in the end.'

The drive was completed in silence, Sue aware of tension in the air. She slipped out of the car as soon as it stopped, thanking Sam and going inside the house as

151

quickly as she could. From her sitting-room window she watched him drive away.

Later, as Sue massaged cream into her winter-dry skin she looked at herself in the mirror. Sam had been completely undemanding, but the evening's message from him she understood. Lifting more cream with her fingers she spread it between her palms, smoothing and kneading away tightness. At first the movements soothed, but Sue was tired and tears of anger prickled.

She rubbed hard, protesting inwardly, not wanting to let go of Colin's part in her life. It was too soon. The rancour eased. Because of Celia Sam knew the need for time. Like Miles he had simply let her know he was waiting.

Baynes, the club in South Molton Street, figured in Cary's column the next day. Wayward royals had decided it was a new watering hole, the cameras on the doorstep an added bonus. Sue waited for the diarist to settle at his desk after what must have been a very good lunch.

'Cary, this place, Baynes.'

'Not thinking of going there, Sue?' Although accompanied by a smile, charm, there was calculation in his eyes.

'No, just curious. Mainly about who's running it.'

'Another dreary piece on salmonella? Not that any prose of yours would be dreary, my dear.'

How did the bimbos put up with him, she wondered?

'Not this time. Why? Is there a risk?'

'With young Rogers in charge of the kitchens? He'd castrate anyone sullying his little empire.'

'What about his boss, Denny Culford?'

'Ah, yes. Young Dennistone. I knew his father. School, you understand. A charming boy Very ambitious.'

'He must be. Does he run the place on his own?'

'He has good staff, I believe.'

'And backers?'

'Sue, what is this? You're as bad as Watty.'

She smiled sweetly, hiding a flare of excitement. 'Watty? Was he interested? What did he want to know?'

The morning had produced a good exclusive and Cary felt expansive. 'He just wanted me to confirm young Culford's major backer. I warn you, Sue. If you want to stick the health and safety boys on to Baynes, you'd better watch yourself on dark nights.'

She laughed. 'It sounds ominous.'

Cary stretched, like a big cat getting ready for sleep after a kill. 'It is, when Paul Chester's involved.'

'Chester? Who's he?'

'Don't ask me, ask Jonah.'

'Chester, you say? Paul Chester? Keep away from him,' Jonah advised before hurrying off. 'As far away as possible.'

Sue headed for the morgue. For once she was in luck. There was only one Paul Chester listed in the cuttings, but a plethora of references to him. She took a deep breath and tapped up the earliest. Fifty words on a court case. A charge of GBH had been abandoned because of witness non-appearance. As she persisted with her search, a pattern began to emerge. Old cases involved Chester directly, but every time the prosecution case fell through. Even in the air scrubbed clean for the computers Sue could smell the stench of fear, of intimidation.

At last there was a photo. It was small, blurred, but muscles stirred deep inside her. More references followed, then a large, clear portrait of a man leaving what looked like an imposing house in the home counties. Stunned, Sue let her hands drop from the keyboard as she gazed at the screen. Back at her looked a man she knew. She had last seen him by the light of a street lamp in Haunch of Venison Yard.

Mr Chester was a man who liked privacy. Sue had driven

slowly past the house in Weybridge, noting the large, solid gates. Turning the car she drove past once more, able to see cameras high on the walls before she parked unobtrusively, ready to watch any comings and goings. One car arrived, the driver speaking into a microphone which descended from an overhead arch. The gates were unlocked electronically, closing swiftly behind the car's tailgate. Automatically, Sue recorded its number.

She did not have long to wait for the next visitor. A low, white sports model shot to a stop. Even from a distance Sue could hear a feminine screech barking orders, followed by the sound of gravel spurting away from the wheels. Two more cars, solid and expensive, passed Sue. She had time to note their numbers before they turned into Chester's driveway. Then there was silence.

Few vehicles troubled her with their passing. It was a quiet road, the houses hidden behind high hedges or walls. The owners were probably all in holiday homes in the sun, she decided as the evening air chilled her muscles.

There was ample time for reflection. What had Chester been doing coming out of a building in Haunch of Venison Yard? Sue picked up her A to Z and turned to the map of South Molton Street, mentally pacing the distances. She must have seen Chester emerging from immediately behind Baynes.

Perhaps he owned the property she had seen him leave, and had made a connection between the two buildings. It would be a good way to get in and out of the South Molton Street club without being spotted by cameramen, but why should he need to if it was a legitimate business?

Baynes had several floors, not all of them used by the restaurant, and Sue passed the time letting her imagination run riot. A brothel at least, she chuckled, but a very upmarket one. Celebrities could be seen going into Baynes, and meet up in privacy on the upper floors. Any extra partners could be secreted in from the back. She must tell Cary, unless he was already a regular patron.

*   *   *

A Range Rover shot past, glossily important, but not interested in the Chesters. Sue lay back and closed her eyes. Had Colin tried to see Chester? It was a possibility, in which case he must have left notes somewhere. 'Be methodical,' she thought. An idea wriggled up.

'Of course!'

Cold and tired, Sue was about to turn the key in the ignition when the gates opened and three cars emerged in quick succession. She peered at the interiors, but could recognize no one. The white coupe did not follow and Sue could only assume it belonged to Chester's wife, Avril. To judge from the newspaper photos she was a very blonde lady, fond of wearing leopard skin in fur or fabric. They looked a couple who deserved each other, she thought, as she slipped the car in gear and drove back to the main road.

As soon as she got home Sue made herself a hot drink, thawing out as she picked up her disks and checked each one. Seven had been discarded before she found the one on which the numbers did not tally. Like the disk on genetic diseases, it had more bytes used than those accounted for by the files listed. Sue felt so stupid for not thinking of this hiding place earlier. Now all she needed was the password. She realized it could be a long evening as she settled to her task.

Chester, Sue thought, it all seemed to centre on him. She tapped in the name and waited. Words rolled on to the screen. In the end, it had all been so simple.

Names appeared, Paul Chester and his Weybridge address at the head of the page. The next two names were of strangers, but the other people Colin had written about were part of the records she had found at the *Journal*.

Sue looked back at the two unknowns. There was a certain familiarity there, but it was not recent. For some reason Ken came to mind, but it was late and Sue was tired. Sleep was claiming her and after printing out a copy of Colin's notes, she crawled into bed, groaning as she thought of the early train she must catch to the Midlands.

It was a good symposium in Nottingham, Sue decided. The train journey up had been fast, and once in the echoing hall of the meeting, she had found friends. It was a day of escapism, Sue able to enjoy the small gossip of lives lived in and around university labs. Here and there she had encountered a snub from someone she had known. Her dereliction from the 'purity of research' was a crime in the eyes of a few. She had smiled, knowing the real gripe was her pay cheque at the end of each month.

Bobby Chalmers had been very patronizing, his new status on a magazine puffing up even further his sense of importance. Sue said little to him, thankful she no longer had to endure him on a daily basis. He had begun to talk disparagingly of Watty, but hands clapped for attention and she could escape and find her seat.

On the journey back to London Sue organized her notes from the lectures. It was quickly done and she tried to think out what must be the next step with Paul Chester, but the rhythm of the train lulled her and she dozed a little, waking with a start when the train stopped and carriages emptied.

London traffic snarled its way around the taxi taking her back to Islington. The driver reached her street at last, and after paying him Sue ran up the stairs to her flat. She felt sticky, jaded, deciding on a shower before she did anything else. The hot water was a benison, sluicing away grime, tiredness. In a towelling robe Sue headed for the kitchen, rubbing her hair dry as she did so. There was a loud knock at the door, the rap of knuckles brooking no delay. Squinting through the peep-hole, Sue saw Stephen. She slipped the chain away and let him in.

'Where the hell have you been?' he demanded.

'Nottingham. Lectures.'

Sue led the way into the sitting room, offering Stephen a drink.

'No – thank you.'

She realized he was angry, and was surprised to see him so. Sue settled on the couch, her feet curled under her, looking like a child wrapped in towelling before a bedtime story.

'Don't you realize what you've been messing in?' he exploded.

She thought of the calm exposition of fairly abstruse research she had listened to all day. 'It's my job,' she told him mildly.

'To go chasing after Chester?' He was clearly furious with her. 'Don't you realize the danger?'

'Who told you?'

'A good friend in one of the Met task forces. Chester is their target and your name came up. Your car had been spotted sitting for hours outside Chester's house in Weybridge.'

'Why tell you?'

'You're listed as Colin's widow and he worked with Ken. After going to him, they came to me to check you out.' In his anger Stephen reached over and caught her shoulders, shaking Sue like a rabbit. 'Don't you realize? If I could get to hear about your stupidity, what about Chester himself? He's got the kind of cash to buy in anywhere. You can bet he knows how far these boys have got keeping tabs on him. For God's sake! He's got the latest surveillance cameras on his gates. He'll have had your number plate checked out before you got to the A3. Your name will have been tossed at him like a juicy bone to a dog!' Fury spent a little, Stephen took a deep breath, rubbing a hand across tired eyes. He looked at Sue, seeing damp hair tousled around a pale face, dark shadows under the eyes. 'I'm sorry.'

'Coffee, or something stronger?'

'I think I need a whisky, but make it a small one. Louise is waiting.'

With glasses in their hands, they sat in front of the fire.

'What put you on to Chester?' Stephen asked.

Sue explained Watty's last day. She told of her hunt through the *Journal's* past issues. Reaching into her briefcase, she pulled out the sheaf of notes and copied articles, then went to her desk to take from a drawer the sheet she had printed the night before.

'That's Colin's notes on him,' she said as she handed him the paper.

Stephen read quickly.

'I couldn't find much about his convictions in our morgue,' Sue added ruefully.

'Chester's very careful never to get caught. Some other poor sucker always gets thrown at us, prepared to do the time.'

'Why?'

'It pays. A spell in jail as Chester's boy guarantees the wife or girlfriend will get their benefits well topped up. Inside, well, he's feared so much, his stooges are very well treated. Outside – no one who wants to stay alive messes with him.'

Sue sipped, reflective. 'And Colin did?'

'I didn't think so, not until your name came up. I've asked Ken for Colin's complete client list, going way back. Someone on it must have dropped a hint which led your husband to Chester's network. It's the most logical explanation.'

'You think Colin went to see Chester?'

'Don't you?'

It was what Sue had tried to do, so she nodded. 'It's likely. Either that or Colin had become obvious by asking awkward questions.'

'And along comes Woolly-hat.'

'Have you found out who he is?' Sue asked.

Stephen shook his head. 'No one has a clue. My guess is he's one of Chester's army.'

'What's Chester's racket?'

Stephen smiled cynically. 'Name it. He oozed up after the Krays went down, taking over part of their empire. That was at first. So, protection, prostitution, supplying whatever's needed. It's only a short step then to funding armed raids, laundering cash and securities. Then there's drugs, of course. They pay too well for him to ignore them, but he's clever. There's never been a scrap of evidence to tie him in directly, yet the finance to swing those deals usually originates from someone close to him. Chester's made sure he never says or writes anything which can be recorded. That's why he's still free.'

There was the quietness after fury, spent emotions. Sue watched the movement of light in the gas fire.

'I think Chester's a silent partner in the new club, Baynes, in South Molton Street,' she said conversationally.

'We knew that.'

'But did you know there may be a back way out of Baynes, through a building in Haunch of Venison Yard?'

'What makes you think so?'

'It's where I bumped into Chester. He came out of a doorway in a hell of a hurry and nearly knocked me flying.'

Stephen groaned. 'He's seen you? Great! That's all we need! I know the Krays made a song and dance about never harming a woman, but Chester's from a new breed. I'll do what I can to get you protection, but it won't be easy.'

The clock on the mantelpiece chimed and Stephen looked at it, alarmed by the hour. 'Look, I've got to go. Lock up behind me carefully. Very carefully. Whatever you do, don't let any strangers in the place. No gas men, council people, no one. Understand?'

Sue nodded, more amused than afraid.

Stephen went off to his Louise, but only after making Sue promise to leave Chester to the police. 'They're chasing him hard, so much so he's begun to make noises about police harassment. It's only a question of time until he's inside.'

After he had gone Sue thought of Stephen's words, his anger. It had been a form of fear, not for himself, but for her. Perhaps he was right. Hounding Chester might give her some satisfaction, but no Colin to hold her.

The answerphone had a message from her mother. Another batch of food was ready for the freezer. Sue switched on her terminal, checking her electronic mail in the office. Paula had written, complaining Beth had sliced her article in half to put in photos. There was a message from Sam, an invitation to Blackheath for Rosalind's fifth birthday party at the weekend. Yawning and ready for her bed, Sue called up the next item. She read it quickly then again, shock paralysing her. The words were few, the message blunt.

'Mind yours, you bitch, unless you want the same as Colin.'

Chapter Nine

'You look a mess. Has something happened?' Kate peered at Sue sitting motionless at her terminal.

'What? Oh, no.'

'Do try to be convincing, for God's sake. You know what this lot's like, they'll smell a rat. Come on. Tell,' Kate commanded.

Sue explained about the message she had received the night before.

'Have you checked your mail today?'

Kate had lost her air of world-weariness and become brusque, efficient. Sue shook her head.

'Do it. Now.'

Sue did as she was told, Kate moving where she could see Sue's screen. There was a request for information as to why DNA testing took so long, a reminder of a press conference to be held next day at the Ministry of Health, jubilation from Anil in Lincolnshire and the information that he would be in later. The screen was blank.

'You couldn't have been imagining it?' Kate wanted to know.

A copy of the missive was in Sue's bag. She took it out and handed it to Kate. 'Who could have done it?'

'Take your pick. Anyone on the paper can find out our passwords if they're clever enough. Then we could have been hacked into. But why should someone be threatening you?'

The photo of Woolly-hat was pulled out and shown to Kate. 'I think he's the one who pushed Colin. There may be a link with a Paul Chester who is, apparently, king of the underworld. The last call Watty had mentioned a link with a Mister Big.'

'After which Watty went out and finished up in Epping Forest,' Kate said softly.

Words began appearing on the blank screen.

'Remember what happened on London Bridge Station? Where do you want it?'

Kate gripped Sue's shoulder. 'Not a word.' Casually, Kate turned and looked around the huge room. She raked each figure for the tell-tale angles which would give away a covert operator. All were as normal, and no one appeared to be the least bit interested in Sue.

'Come on,' Kate ordered. 'We're going to see Sam.'

Although she protested, Sue found herself seated in Sam's office.

'There's no need for me to be here,' Sue protested.

'If our system's being used for hate mail, I want to know about it,' Sam insisted, his jaw jutting. 'This is my paper, and whoever thinks this sort of thing clever I will fire and blacklist.'

'How can you trace them?' Sue asked. 'They could have phoned it in.'

'We pay bloody fortunes to computer whizz kids. They can find out or get sacked themselves.'

'But why should anyone use this way?' Kate asked.

'Everyone's an expert at committing crimes these days. Even a baby knows the source of phone calls can be identified, faxes too. Letters, well, forensic specialists can get proof of the writer. All anyone needs for this type of crime is Sue's password,' Sam informed her brusquely.

'What is it?' Kate wanted to know.

'SBSCIENCE,' Sam answered bitterly. 'Her initials and her job. A ten-year-old could crack that in thirty seconds.' He turned to Sue. 'Go back to your desk, and take Kate with you. Kate, can you spill coffee on to Sue's keyboard and terminal?'

162

'If you think it's a good idea.' A twinkle appeared in her eyes.

'Not too much of a grand performance, if you don't mind. Just enough to give a reason why Sue's terminal's out of action.'

'The one at home?' Sue queried.

'I'll send someone round.' Sam dialled a number on the internal phone system and gave his name. 'Get here. Now!'

As Kate and Sue left the office a lanky figure with a flop of curls and dreamy eyes hurried in.

'Julian's on the job, I see,' Kate remarked as she and Sue went back to their desks. 'He's supposed to be the best in Wapping.'

'Then I hope he's not the one making my life hell,' Sue sighed.

'Aren't you getting a teensy bit paranoid?' Kate inquired acidly, but she put an arm round Sue as she said it, the contact reassuring.

Sue sat at her desk sorting papers, filling her waste bin. Was she getting obsessed? It was the thought of someone whose face she did not know watching her, waiting for her to be vulnerable. As she sat engrossed in her thoughts, Kate arrived with a cup of coffee and gave a faultless demonstration of an accident. The coffee covered a wide arc. Sue's terminal and keyboard got their full share, as did Kate's suit.

Work ended for Sue, being scooted off home by Kate who left at the same time to get her suit treated while the stains were still fresh.

'Actually darling,' she confided to Sue, 'it needed cleaning. This way the *Journal* can pay for it!'

'You must tell Stephen,' Pippa insisted. Sue had gone upstairs to Pippa's flat while she waited for Julian to arrive and organize a trace on any unofficial traffic through the terminal in the flat below.

'I suppose so. He won't be pleased.'

'He'll be furious, but not at you. Don't forget, the more contact anyone tries to make, the more clues they leave behind.'

'You've been talking to him,' Sue accused.

'Of course. He was here for ages the other evening, waiting for you to come back from Nottingham. Three times he called Louise. She must have the patience of a saint. Have you ever met her?'

'No. Stephen doesn't like her getting to know people involved in any of his cases. She's a sensitive, psychic, if you like.'

Pippa shivered. 'No thank you.'

'I've got to do something. Come and have lunch with me. I've still got enough to feed an army.'

'Ooh, good. I am hungry. No time for breakfast this morning.'

'Was it Dennis Dormouse, or one of Ken's shirts that needed ironing?' Sue grinned as she beat a hasty retreat from a flung cushion.

The phone was ringing as she went back into her flat. Hurrying across the room Sue lifted the receiver only to hear the dialling tone. 'Damn,' she said softly, then made for the kitchen, emptying lunch possibles on the counter to make choice easier. The phone rang again. Once more the line was disconnected as soon as the ringing ceased. Annoyed, Sue selected lamb stew, scalloped potatoes, green beans. With the first package thawing in the microwave, the phone bell trilled, but now the handset was in the kitchen and Sue switched it on. Immediately the caller cut the connection.

By the time Sue had lunch ready for Pippa the mystery caller had tried twice more, each time breaking off as soon as she answered the phone.

'If you can't ignore it, turn the damned thing off,' Pippa advised.

Sue accepted the advice, pulling the plug from the wall.

Lunch was heated, eaten, enjoyed. With coffee mugs to hand Sue and Pippa stretched out in the sitting room.

'This is nice –' Pippa began when Sue's mobile phone buzzed.

Before Sue could get to it, the noise ceased. Deep inside her she felt a tremor of fear. The phone buzzed a second time, the ringing lasting seconds only. The tremor became a shiver.

'The mobile number's ex-directory. Whoever's doing it knows all about me.'

'Ring Stephen now,' Pippa ordered and got up to find the brandy bottle, sloshing a generous dollop into Sue's mug.

Stephen was out. He would be informed of the message as soon as he returned to the station, Sue was told by a calm voice with Liverpudlian overtones. She sipped her coffee absentmindedly.

'Now what?'

'Try your editor. The *Journal* pays for the phone, doesn't it? So it's his problem.'

The door bell rang, and Sue tensed. Pippa went to the peephole. 'It's a tall, skinny bod. He looks as though he's half asleep.'

Sue went to look, then sighed with relief. 'It's only Julian.'

The computer expert was armed with a shapeless hold-all, odd protrusions indicating hasty packing. He headed for the terminal, nodding approval when he saw it had been unplugged.

'Lunch, Julian?'

Soft brown curly hair swung as he turned to peer at Sue. 'Lunch?'

'Have you eaten?'

He thought carefully for a moment. 'No.'

'Would you like something?'

He frowned, concentrating on the question. 'I think so. Later.'

As Sue went to the kitchen Pippa was stifling giggles,

but they stopped when Julian began handling the computer equipment. Like a surgeon he inserted wires, connectors, a small box. By the time Sue returned carrying a tray he was packing up his gear.

'Leave it switched on. All communications can be identified.'

'How?' Pippa wanted to know.

The dreamy eyes sharpened, focussing as he looked at her. 'Trade secret.'

'Do you have any for mobile phones?' Sue asked him.

Julian let his food get cold as he listened to her explanation. He thought long and hard, his forehead ridged with furrows.

'No,' he said simply then picked up his fork.

Stephen appeared at Sue's as daylight was waning. 'Right. Bring me up to date.'

Sue did so, giving him a clear, concise account of all that had happened.

'Any more messages on that thing?' He nodded at the terminal.

'No. I can only guess someone knew Julian had been put on the job.'

'If it blocks your pest's use of the computers, great,' Stephen decided. 'The phones?'

'When I do plug the phone in, the calls start up again. As for the mobile, it's switched off and under a pile of pillows in the wardrobe.' She shivered, then hugged herself for warmth. 'It's as though someone is watching my every move.'

'Can you get the phone in action? Then I can use it.'

Sue did as he asked. Almost immediately the bell rang, stopping as Stephen put the phone to his ear.

'I see what you mean. Never mind, let's try a call out.'

The phone company were prepared to be helpful, but it would take time, he was told. Sue and Pippa saw Stephen's face harden. Crisply, with not a wasted word, he gave orders as to the work to be done and the delay acceptable to him. By the time Stephen had finished with them, the delay was to be minimal before Mrs Bennett had a new number. In the meantime an operator would monitor all calls.

The mobile phone had to be dragged from its nest. It was silent. 'If it's been unanswered, they no doubt assume you've switched off or left it in the car.' Stephen got through to the operator then the supervisor, repeating his request. It was simpler to accommodate him this time, and again all calls would be checked.

'Whoever's behind this probably has an informant at the *Journal*.' Stephen accepted a mug of coffee from Pippa. He sipped the hot liquid gratefully, then smiled at Sue. 'It wouldn't be too hard to see you react this morning. You and What's-her-name going to see the editor and then coffee all over your machine.'

'I thought it all looked very natural,' Sue protested.

'It would to your average Joe Soap, but to someone watching you for signals? After that had been passed on to whoever's behind it all, they probably assumed, quite rightly, it was no use getting at you through the computer system. I presume your address and phone numbers would be in personnel files?'

'I imagine so,' Sue said. 'You mean they've got into those?'

'Without a doubt. There are some damned good hackers about at the moment, and they're an immoral lot.'

'How can you say that?' Pippa protested.

'Easily,' Stephen assured her. 'Stealing information belonging to someone else is theft, just like any other kind. These days a hacker can enjoy himself, or herself, and get paid for it.'

'Who would pay for it?'

'It could be anyone. Colin stuck his nose into a very large beehive. There's enough honey there to buy most people.'

Sue tried to think logically. 'If they can afford to pay for killing Colin and Watty . . .'

'Scaring you doesn't come very expensive,' he said softly. 'Can't you get away?'

The adrenaline of fear began to ebb, flowing back as anger. 'Why should I?'

'Because of what happened to Colin.'

She looked at him. 'Am I in that kind of danger?'

Stephen's look was direct, uncompromising. 'I don't know, but it's possible. And yet . . .'

'What is it?'

'Colin had no warnings?'

Sue searched her memory for any clue, seeing Colin's face, his smile, no sense of danger. She shook her head.

'And as far as is known, neither did Skinner.' Stephen took her hands, trying to warm confidence in her. 'If Chester wanted you right out of the way, there would have been no warnings. We'd have been to your funeral by now.'

She laughed, the sound shaky in the twilight. 'You do have a way of making a girl feel better.'

With the computer made safe and her phone calls sifted, Sue began to ease muscles stiff with tension. Hot showers, hot-water bottles in her bed did the trick, as did Pippa and Ken, waltzing into the flat with huge Chinese take-aways and soft wine. Sleep followed, each night eating away at the bank of fatigue which had built up. After a week or so Kate noticed the improvement.

'Give, darling,' she ordered.

'What?'

'You're trying out some new mineral supplement. What is it? Zinc? I thought it was only used for baths and buckets.'

'Kate, what on earth are you drivelling on about?'

'You. You look so much more – you.'

Sue chuckled. 'A hot-water bottle and bedsocks. They're great for a good night's sleep.'

'My God! That's blasphemy! Girls who wear bedsocks have to sleep alone!'

'I do, remember?' Sue said, but without rancour.

Jonah joined them, carrying a sheet of paper. 'Do what?'

'Sleep.'

'A lot more people will after tomorrow,' he said with satisfaction.

'Any special reason?' Sue asked.

He flourished the rough proof of the next day's front page. 'We got the exclusive.'

Sue saw a familiar face pictured on a yacht slipping its mooring. 'Paul Chester.'

'That's the lad. Peter Tym got shots of him in Dorset, heading out for a day's sailing. What we didn't know until last night was that he made straight for France, then a private jet to Spain. He's holed up on the Costa del Crime. Silly bugger,' he added with sly glee. 'Now Spain's in the EC, extradition's more likely.'

'What triggered him into running?' Sue wanted to know.

'Scotland Yard had him in their sights. I expect he has someone there on the payroll. With that sort of early-warning system it meant he got out before they felt his collar.'

'Leaving some poor sucker to do his time,' Sue quoted softly.

'What was that?' Kate sensed a story.

'Just something someone said about him,' Sue said.

She stretched, her muscles rippling like those of a cat. 'You're right, Jonah.' Sue pointed to the copy. 'A lot of people will sleep easier when they've seen that.' She would be one of them.

Rosalind's party had been a great success, the children eating enormously when not involved in games devised by their father and Sam. While Peter's tended to be ones which needed mental effort, Sam organized forays in the garden and over furniture, causing a lot of noise and a great deal of laughter.

Sam looked years younger, jacket and tie discarded, while Rosalind and Phoebe took turns in riding him around the sitting room. He was the willing horse when it was time for the girls to go upstairs to bed.

Sue was surprised how well Sam played with children, having none of his own.

'Too busy making his way,' Celia explained. 'His father died when he was ready to graduate. The day before, actually,' she reminisced. 'From then on he did his damnedest to help his mother bring up the rest. Instead of going on to do his Master's he got a job on the local paper. It must have been hard going, feeding and clothing all of them on a cub reporter's pay, but he did it.'

Sue had seen the skill with which Sam held Phoebe while fending off Adam and two little buddies. 'Yes, I can imagine he would.'

'How about you?' Celia asked. 'Have you family?'

'Brothers and sisters have I none,' Sue laughed. 'I'm the only child, but I do have both my parents still.' She crossed fingers as she spoke, frightened of tempting Providence.

'Sam tells me you were a zoologist originally. Why journalism?'

'A fight with an editor of a local paper when I was at university. I tore strips off him for allowing total inaccuracies to be printed in a story. He asked me if I could do better myself.'

Celia offered Sue some biscuits, only the plain ones left from the children's depredations. 'And you could?'

'He printed it, with very little subbing, and took me on part-time. I suppose I got hooked.'

'And the zoology?'

'It's still there.'

'Good. The children have asked to go to the zoo in Regent's Park again. You'll just have to come with us. Adam keeps asking questions about the animals neither

Peter nor I can cope with. Having you with us would be great – on all counts!'

Sue was not surprised when Sam accompanied them. The gleam in Celia's eyes had warned her. It was a pleasant day, the children awed at first, then hurrying from compound to compound, seeing the personalities inside and not beasts caged for their enjoyment.

As always, Sue was drawn to the orang-utans, the quiet dam amongst them expressing her thoughts in her eyes. Silently Sue communed with the proud female, each realizing the hurt deep in the other until a brightly coloured baby climbed up its mother's legs seeking food. At the feel of the infant, the orang-utan's eyes softened and she bent to hoist the hungry mouth to her breast.

Suddenly bereft, Sue turned away, only then realizing Sam had been watching her. She flushed, embarrassed her thoughts might have been naked on her face. Sam linked his arm through hers.

'Adam says he's starving and Rosalind says will you tell her why elephants have such long noses?'

Sue had another two days of relief before the hated calls began again. The first one had a voice. Gravelly, full of hatred, 'You can't hide from me, you bitch,' exploded in her ear. Then he cursed, only a few of the expletives familiar. The first shock was a long time evaporating. Sue was numb, the abuse flowing round her as she stood paralysed. The caller used Colin's name and it triggered Sue into action. She began to come alive again, reaching for the police whistle Ken had insisted she keep by the phone. After one good, long blast into the speaker she listened. The caller had gone.

It felt wonderful to have hit back, but more practical to start making arrangements for yet another number. Sue was doing that when Pippa arrived at the door.

171

'I heard the whistle. Trouble?'

Sue nodded. 'I've just been told most pests give up in time, but I want him caught.'

'So do I,' Pippa agreed, 'and castrated.'

Sue laughed, the sound a little shaky 'A bit drastic?'

'Not at all. He'd make a dreadful father.'

Pippa followed Sue into the kitchen and watched her move washing from the machine to the dryer. 'You've reminded me I've a load of Ken's shirts to do. Why do solicitors have to wear so many shirts?'

'They don't. Just like everyone else, they can only wear one at a time.'

'You know what I mean,' Pippa growled.

Sue did. She remembered past impatience at all the ironing and sighed, wishing the chore was hers again.

'Did you say you were going to Bristol in the morning?'

Sue filled the kettle. 'Yes. There's a conference I need to go to, and a couple of friends to see. I should be back by midnight.'

Pippa chuckled. 'Just don't lose your glass slipper, Cinderella.'

Sue was not sure when she realized she was being followed. From Bristol's Temple Meads Station she had taken a taxi to the imposing hotel on College Green where industrialists were to talk to university researchers. It was only later she remembered the deep-set eyes of the man staring at her from a passing taxi as she paid off her driver.

On the train back to London Sue was engrossed in a book Pippa had insisted she read. It was a good story and she was unaware of other passengers moving past her. As the train slowed for its run into Paddington, Sue felt the hairs on the back of her neck move. It was a frisson from life in prehistoric jungles, when a sixth sense had warned of unseen dangers.

As she stood, ready for the train to stop at the platform, Sue casually looked around the compartment. Most passengers were standing, sleepily watching the platform slide past. Near the far door a man sat reading a paper, holding it high with thick fingers. Above the newsprint Sue could see the peak of a baseball cap. As she was about to leave the train and head for a waiting taxi, the paper was lowered, revealing eyes fixed on her. Sue recognized them. She ran.

The drive to Islington was uneventful, but as Sue alighted outside her home, a second taxi crawled past hers. She could not see the passenger, but she knew she was not imagining the stare.

Safely locked inside the flat Sue began to shake. Waves of fear washed over her, abating only as time passed and the shivering of her muscles brought warmth. She reached for the phone to dial Pippa's number, only remembering then that Pippa was with Ken and out of London.

Sue thought of Stephen. She pressed his numbers with shaking fingers, but stopped halfway. What could she tell him? That she had been followed to Bristol and back? No one was to be seen in the street and there was nothing Stephen could do except reassure. He was a busy man and Sue knew it was not fair to demand his time. Her fears must be faced and endured alone.

Only when the TV bored her beyond reason did Sue go to bed. When she did lie in the dark the hot-water bottle she cradled for comfort gradually cooled and it was a very long time before she slept.

Next morning there was an envelope sticking out of the mailbox. Sue's name and address had been typed, but there was no stamp. Inside was a single sheet of paper with 'NOWHERE TO HIDE', the mechanical letters sharp with venom.

Relief quickly followed shock. She had not imagined last night's shadower and at last there was something tangible to show Stephen. She went back to the flat to contact him.

At that hour he was already at his desk. 'Hang on to it, Sue,' he advised when she had told him of the hand-delivered letter. 'You know the drill. Don't handle it any more than you have done already in case there are prints. I'll collect it tonight.'

'I don't think there's much you can do.'

'No,' Stephen agreed, 'but there's a lot you can. Make sure you take no risks, and keep alert for anything which could help identify a possible tail. Having said that, the letter is probably only extra pressure, scaring you so you leave the Chester business alone. That's not a bad idea, you know. Just go off to work, and forget about it.'

It was easier said than done, but Sue arrived at the *Journal* office with both her determination and a smile fixed firmly in place. After checking mail and memos, Sue was about to start work. 'Sandy!' she called.

Small, dark, intense, Sandy Jackson stopped at Sue's desk. 'Something for me?' he asked, quirking an eyebrow at her over his glasses.

'Possibly. A friend I talked to yesterday. She's very concerned about BIV.'

'Sounds painful.'

'It is – if you're a cow. Wobbly legs, runny nose, scabs. The calves literally curl up and die. It's caused by a bovine immuno-deficiency virus.'

'Sounds like AIDS.'

Sue nodded. 'It's become recognized as bovine AIDS and it's been imported into Britain.'

Sandy's eyes gleamed suddenly 'Ah! From Germany?'

'In Holstein cows bought from Holland, but they had gone there from Germany. The disease has wiped out one British herd already.'

Fingers drumming on Sue's computer punctuated Sandy's thoughts, then he smiled, stretching like a replete cat. 'We can't stop the animals coming in without getting thumped by the EC, unless . . .'

He looked at Sue. She nodded, her answering grin infectious. 'Unless', she finished for him, 'the Germans have already trampled that regulation out of existence by banning our beef. If they insist on doing that, we can stop them sending us their rotten stock.'

'Sue, you're an angel!'

'There's more.'

Sandy cast his eyes heavenwards. 'It must be my birthday.' He turned to Sue. 'Go on, spoil me.'

'Britain's been free of brucellosis, but it's coming back in, the same way as the rest of the bugs.'

'Yippee!'

Startled neighbours turned away from their work and watched as Sandy hugged Sue, kissing the top of her head.

'Do me the facts, will you, Sue? Spellings, and so on?'

Smiling, she handed him a sheet of paper, the data ready for him. 'How are the twins?'

Sandy stilled, looking intently at Sue. She knew his daughters had been born the day Colin died. Sandy had never talked to her of them, strangely ashamed of his great happiness when Sue had lost so much. She looked at him serenely, waiting for his answer.

'They are so beautiful,' he said gently. 'Thank God they're beginning to sleep better at night. It means we can, too.'

'No photographs?'

Almost shyly, he produced snapshots and Sue made the appropriate responses before Sandy went off to write a blistering attack on the EC apparently encouraging a wide variety of diseases to be imported into Britain.

It had been a busy day in the office, but one of those when demands could be met and a sense of satisfaction achieved. To top it all there had been a phone call for Sam from a laboratory. The director had been thrilled by a large and anonymous donation, and all because Sue, the spokesman insisted, had written up a little-known piece of research into regeneration of nerve tissue.

In Islington that evening Sue parked her car and collected her possessions. Locking the car door she was about to turn and go up the steps to her home when she froze, the back of her neck prickling. Someone was watching her. She had not been aware of any stranger in the street, but instinct had flared again, strong, primitive.

With an effort she stood erect and casually glanced round. There was no one in sight. Forcing herself to walk steadily Sue went home and locked herself in the flat, going to the window which faced the street before putting on any lights. Immobile, she waited. After what seemed an eternity, a figure slipped out of a doorway and went to a small van halfway along the road. It was difficult to see clearly, but she was sure it was not the man from the train.

There was an overwhelming urge to talk to someone, but who? Her parents would be alarmed and probably call out the police. Pippa had taken Ken to visit her godmother and was still in Devon. Sue looked at the empty couch. It was in her power to have Sam sitting there, or Miles, but to ask either of them for their company would be giving out signals she was not yet ready to send. There was no alternative but to wait for Stephen. She was restless until he came.

'I can't stay long,' he apologized.

'It's good of you to come,' Sue assured him, hoping her relief was not too obvious. 'I put the envelope and the letter in plastic bags, but I can't see they'll give you much information.'

'Maybe not, but they're evidence, and every little helps.' He smiled at Sue. 'Don't let it get to you. I'll have a word with your local nick and ask them to keep an eye on this place. There's no sign anyone wants to harm you physically. I know it's been foul, but all you've experienced has been intimidation, so I can't do much more. It's up to you to act sensibly and keep your head. Make a record of anything that happens,' he suggested.

When Stephen left fear returned, flickering at the edges

176

of Sue's mind. She pushed it away, trying to think logically. Martin Lawrence had not wanted her frightened, and Watty had made sure the invasions of her flat had been as discreet as possible. That was in the past. Now she was caught and held by the tentacles of a very different animal, this one as unseen as it was deadly. This time there was no Watty to protect her.

Watty. Sue closed her eyes, remembering his smile and feeling the warmth of his personality. Like Martin Lawrence he had worked for a natural justice. Their gatherings had debated fairly, Colin's notes had made that clear.

Chester was different. His organization had the stench of a dictatorship, the justice he dealt in merely a commodity to be bought. There was no assessment of right and wrong, only of the amount of money to be made, with Chester's greed the deciding factor.

Stephen was right, Sue decided. If she was in physical danger, Chester's men would not have bothered to waste time frightening her.

The rational part of her mind made her prepare for bed calmly. She drew the curtains and switched on the lights. The door was checked, the chain in place, she was safe. When Sue did sleep it was fitfully, waking often bathed in sweat, her pulses racing.

Next morning there was no van and no perception of threat. In the busy *Journal* offices Sue forgot her panic.

Sam sent for her. 'We've got the bastard.' He was grimly triumphant. 'The mole.'

'Who is it?'

'Eamon Doyle.'

Sue conjured up a nondescript face, thin, sharp-nosed. 'Isn't he part of Meg's team?'

'Was. Julian caught him accessing a set of data which looked odd. Turns out it was company tax records.'

'And you wouldn't want those published.'

'I'll have you know ours can bear anyone's scrutiny. Well, almost anyone's.' Sam sat back in his chair, swinging it like a small boy enjoying himself. 'They weren't from our files, but some of Jepson's private holdings, and nothing to do with the *Journal*. Doyle was just using our system to get enough on Jepson for blackmail. When I asked him if he was moonlighting for Chester as well, he just smiled at me and said, "Prove it." Thanks to Julian, I did, to my satisfaction, anyway.'

'Was he a freelance before he came here?' Sue vaguely remembered one of Cary's blondes complaining about the 'nasty little Dubliner'.

'A staff reporter on the *Spokesman*. I can see why Bill Wolfit got shot of him, but not why we got such glowing references for him.'

'Perhaps he'd tried the same trick there and had the dirt on someone high up,' Sue suggested.

'I'm afraid you could be right.' Sam grinned, his eyes cold. 'Well, he's gone and I'll black him for certain.'

'With a name like that you'd better watch out for the IRA,' Sue laughed before going back to her desk.

Only as she prepared to return home did Sue wonder if the previous day's panic would return. Once inside the flat she should be safe from the intimidating phone calls now Chester's men no longer had a way of finding out her new numbers. Julian, bless him, had ensured her computers remained private, and Stephen had taken the letter away for testing. Every angle had been covered.

Sue was not able to relax. Even if there were no more precautions to be taken, it was still disturbing to be the object of someone's intense scrutiny

Concentrating on getting through the evening rush-hour traffic made Sue forget her problems for a while, until she turned off into her street. It was quiet, dark. Stepping out on to the pavement Sue waited for the back of her neck to warn her. Nothing. With increasing confidence she went towards the front door. She was nearly there when she felt eyes boring into her back. A rush of steps and she was at the front door, closing it behind her with a slam.

Once inside the flat Sue slid the chain across, only then

178

daring to release breath. When her heart stopped racing and was returning to a normal beat she went to the window, standing in darkness behind the curtains to scan the street below.

From her window she could see nothing, then a car edged out into the road and towards the main road, driven very slowly past her building. Although there was no reason to suspect the driver, it took many deep breaths to achieve equanimity.

It was time to think rationally and not like a victim. Paul Chester had been the source of her problems. He was out of the country, hiding to save his own skin, Sue assured herself firmly. When she went to bed she piled dull books beside her, one of which should drive her into oblivion.

During the next few days, and too often for her peace of mind, Sue experienced the tinglings which heralded the knowledge she was being watched. It happened as she left her flat, when she was coming out of the *Journal* offices at lunchtime, unlocking her car door ready to drive home, occasionally in traffic, wondering which of the drivers behind was the shadower.

Sue could find no pattern to the harassment, each man she glimpsed yet another stranger. She recorded what information she could, but there was little that made sense.

Stephen rang and confirmed what Sue had guessed. No clues had been left on the warning note. 'The local boys have agreed to do what they can. Apart from that, all I can do is get a message through informers suggesting you be left well alone,' he said. 'With Chester out of the country it might work.'

Whether it was the passage of time or Stephen's efforts was not clear, but the trailing stopped. Sue's exhilaration increased as she was able to go to and from work without fear. Meeting Miles for a meal was something to anticipate with pleasure, as was joining Sam on a visit to Blackheath and the happy noise of the children.

On a Friday evening Sue pulled into the huge, well-lit car-park of a supermarket. Pushing her trolley through the lofty arcades she had a sense of release, freedom. It lasted all through her shopping expedition, right up until she had filled the car's boot and was preparing to heave her trolley back in line with dozens of others. Turning quickly, she bumped into a customer. Looking up to apologize she recognized him in the strong lighting. Under a flat cap fringed by reddish curls was the face of the man who had pushed Colin to his death.

With a gasp she stepped back. The man glared at her, his deep-set eyes glinting.

'You had to stick your effing nose in, you stupid cow. Buggered everything up.' His south London voice was harsh with fury.

He was ready to launch another attack, but small boys had been attracted by the noise, sensing a fight. They began to gather, bright-eyed, eager for the sensation of what they hoped would be a brawl. The man could not risk so many witnesses and stormed off.

Frozen to the spot Sue watched him walk away. People milled round her, tutting because she impeded them in their search for trolleys.

'Are you all right?'

Her questioner was small, stout, middle-aged.

'Thank you, yes. I'm fine. I just had a shock.'

'Why not go into the café and have a hot drink? It will do you good. I'll come with you, if it's any help.'

'No, I don't want anything, but thank you,' she added, grateful for the grey-haired woman's concern. 'I have to make a phone call.'

This time she did not hesitate to ring Stephen. A woman's voice answered, telling her Stephen would be home soon, and asking if she could take a message.

'Tell him it's Sue. Woolly-hat has been following me. I've just bumped into him and he spoke to me.'

There was a strange silence, then, 'Sue, this is Louise. Don't go home.'

The urgency in the tones startled Sue. 'Why not?'

'I don't know, but please,' Louise begged, 'go somewhere you can be safe.'

Sue remembered how she and Pippa had been entertained by the idea of practical Stephen with a girlfriend who was psychic. It was no longer amusing. 'I'll go to Dorking,' she said quietly.

'It's a sizeable town, I suppose, but can you be sure it's safe?' Louise sounded doubtful.

'Why do you ask?' Sue hoped she had managed to keep the shaking from her voice.

'I don't know. There's no real reason. Just be careful,' Louise begged.

If her parents were surprised to see Sue, they gave no hint of it. After hugging her with delight they unpacked her groceries, and hurried her into the house and a meal.

'Everything OK, darling?' her father asked when his wife was seeing to Sue's bed.

'Fine. I just had the urge to come here for a change.'

'Well, it is Friday. That's the best night to get away for a weekend break. You can stay all weekend?'

She smiled at his pleasure in her visit. 'Of course.'

Sleep was difficult in the quiet house, in spite of her old pyjamas and nearby teddy bear. Sue heard the grandfather clock chime the small hours before she dozed off, waking at the sound of her father creeping downstairs to make tea for his wife. Sue dressed quickly and followed him. It was warm in the kitchen, the tea hot and strong.

There was energy in Sue's muscles, an urge for exercise: 'I'll go for a walk, I think,' she told her father. 'It's always good when the day's just waking up.'

'Your boots are in the scullery cupboard.' He smiled apologetically 'I'm afraid your mother insisted on washing them, but I got some dubbin to 'em, so no harm's done.'

The walking boots which had carried Sue for miles were unharmed by their bath, indeed there were new laces in the eyelets. The morning outdoors was crisp, a hint of mist carrying the aroma of last night's bonfires. Sue strode off, the sense of freedom exhilarating.

Over the common she went, stopping once to retie a bootlace. There was no one else in view, not even the earliest of the dog-walkers. Sue decided to go home through the copse alongside the stream. It had been a favourite place when she had been small, the dappling on a summer's day enchanting, the wildlife under the stones of the stream fascinating. This morning was no exception, but she was hungry and did not wait to investigate old friends.

The trees were thinning out, thick shrubs replacing them as she walked steadily on. One ankle was uncomfortable and she looked down. 'Damn,' she breathed, and bent to tie up the loose lace. Her mitts she dropped on the grass beside her as she prepared to deal with cotton made slippery by the greasy dubbin.

Only as she began to stand upright was she aware of the figure behind her. Strong hands went round her throat, frustrated a little by the neck of her sweater. Within seconds Sue was fighting for her life.

'You bitch!' she heard, in amongst abuse she could not recognize. Dimly, she heard, 'Your effing old man was trouble, but I did for 'im, and I'll do for you.'

There was a vicious twist of the hands. The man's grunts of effort came thinly through the throbbing in her head. Sue was in a darkening world. Was she really going to die?

Anger suffused through the panic. Tensing her neck muscles, she tore with her nails at the hands choking the life out of her. Sue tried to twist round, aiming a knee at the man's groin. The angle made it impossible for her to ram him as hard as she would have liked, but it was enough to do some damage.

The pain made him ease his hold and she drew in a

ragged, gasping breath before he roared and increased the pressure. The oxygen she had gained gave her a split second to think and she gouged at where his eyes must be, almost recoiling from the feeling of soft vulnerability into which she thrust her nails.

Sue was vaguely aware she had been flung on the ground. She tried to breathe, but it hurt too much. Like a doll she was picked up by her jacket and dragged to the stream, dumped in the water face down, a heavy foot across the back of her head.

Sue was choking, water in her nose, her mouth. There was a singing in her ears, and somewhere a dog barked faintly in the ever-deepening darkness.

Chapter Ten

Voices were pulling Sue awake. There was light, then noise. She tried to turn her head away and hide, but it hurt. The fire of pain grew and raced through her, overwhelming her like surf as it rose and choked. A bee stung her arm. Sue wanted to cry out, but no words would come. Her eyelids were too heavy to lift and she gave herself to the darkness. As Sue began to float free, the pain which had been drowning her was dragged back to the shallows.

The next time Sue became conscious of her surroundings she heard her mother's voice. 'It's all right, darling. Daddy and I are here.'

Sue tried to turn her head, frightened when she found herself unable to move.

'Keep still, Poppet. The nurses have ice packs round your throat. In a day or so the swellings will be down and you can wriggle as much as you like.' Her father's deep tones were reassuring.

Sue struggled to open her eyes, but the lids were too heavy to lift. 'How?' she said, but no sound came.

Her mother had read her lips. 'It was Mrs Willoughby who got to you. Hector went to the stream barking like mad and she followed. She frightened the man away and got you out in time.'

'Thank God,' her father added in amen.

'Caught?' Sue tried, but silently.

'Yes. They've got him.' There was no mistaking the relish in her father's voice.

Sue sighed and slept.

Days and nights were jumbled together, punctuated by rustling nurses with full plastic bottles to replace the ones which had been fed into Sue's arm. Doctors came, talked quietly, cheerfully, and went. Her parents chatted to Sue now and again, encouraging her to sleep. She tried to tell them it was hard to stay awake, but her consciousness slid away before she could mouth the words.

There were times when pain held Sue, forcing her to hear again and again how lucky she was, that there would be a few days of discomfort but she would be as good as new. She longed for deep sleep but dreaded the price of its dreams. Sedation must suffice, a chemical limbo in which Sue's body healed and her mind gradually accepted the harsh reality of what had happened.

'Alopecia,' Mrs Willoughby said firmly.

Sue was sitting up and receiving visitors carefully selected by the policewoman at the door. Mrs Willoughby had discarded her body-warmer for a heather tweed suit of impeccable cut, but she had not been allowed to bring Hector, the real hero of the day.

'I grabbed for his hair, always upsetting for a man to have his hair tugged hard. Such a surprise when it all came away in my hands. There he was, his bald head shining like a billiard ball. I thumped him good and hard, and Hector bit him. It was all we could manage, I'm afraid. Too important getting you out.'

Sue had a strange memory of air being forced in her mouth.

'Had to give you the kiss of life, m'dear. Do hope you don't mind.'

Various policemen and women of the Surrey force peopled the little ward, tiring Sue with questions about James Rocket, a man she had known as Woolly-hat. Speech was still difficult. It was easier to wave a hand and close her eyes, halting the interview. The police persisted, proffering a note-pad and pencil with determined courtesy.

Writing exhausted her, but Sue fought tiredness to find out that once the police knew of the alopecia Rocket had been quickly located and detained. Sue's scratching had striped his hands, and the torn skin from under her nails would give DNA proof in time. Until then, a CID man grinned, they would have to make do with Hector's teeth marks.

Nurses came to shoo away the officials, but finally Stephen was beside the bed.

'Why?' she wrote, her eyes pleading.

'Do you remember the man Colin was defending? The one with the grandson threatened by a pitbull terrier?'

Sue nodded, wincing.

'When Colin first saw his client in the cells, the teenager at the root of the problem was in the station. Colin heard him threaten the old man that once he was inside, the weasels would get him.'

There was puzzlement in Sue's frown.

'I used an informant who owed me a favour,' Stephen went on. 'He chatted up the lad, Terry McAteer, a real boastful little runt who wants to kid everyone he's hard, one of the big boys. Terry couldn't wait to let on how much he knew. The weasel isn't the animal, it's a sharp tool for punching holes in leather and felt. Hatters used to use it. "Pop goes the weasel"?'

A nurse hustled in and poured a drink for Sue, a child's bendy straw to help her.

Sue sucked patiently then lay back. 'Go on,' her lips urged Stephen.

'Chester had his own system in the jails, dishing out what he called justice. We've known that all along. Anyone who offended Chester got the treatment. The more upset he was, the harder they were hit. We suspected Chester's boys took on extra duties, helping to settle scores for others – providing, of course, the price was right. McAteer laid it all out for us.'

Stephen looked anxiously at Sue. She tried a smile to reassure him she was still awake and listening.

'If you wanted a revenge killing,' he went on, 'or a beating, all you had to do was go into Chester territory and talk about weasels. After you'd been checked out, you'd be contacted, and your job done for you. Cash up front.'

Sue reached for her pencil and pad, writing swiftly. 'Baynes, South Molton Street. Chester going upmarket?'

Stephen read and nodded agreement. 'Very democratic chap, our Paul Chester.' His smile was wintry and did not reach his eyes. 'He believed the rich were entitled to justice as well. Besides, they would pay better than the poor.'

'Why kill Colin?' The whisper was harsh, difficult.

'Chester must have found out your husband was on his trail. He probably guessed no threat or cash would ever work on Colin, and he must also have guessed Colin was on to his very profitable weasel system. It was odds on your husband would have blown the whole business wide open. Chester couldn't afford that. He had Colin stopped.'

Stopped by a train at London Bridge Station, Sue thought. She was washed with agony yet again, the feeling deadened by sedatives.

'We can't prove it,' Stephen went on, 'but there's no doubt your friend Watson Skinner got close to the proof of Chester's involvement in Colin's murder. It wouldn't have taken a genius to realize there was no bribe big enough to buy off Skinner.'

The shallow grave in Epping Forest was in both their minds.

'Rocket?' The word was firm, scoring the paper.

'Banged up, tight as a drum. No bail.'

Sue was tired, her lids closing of their own volition. Stephen touched her hand gently and left.

Consciousness was drifting away and Sue was bathed in the warm glow of safety A thought wriggled like a worm through the onrushing sleep. Safe while Rocket was locked away.

She woke to the perfume of flowers. Next to the bed a Chinese nurse was setting up a sphygmomanometer. A thermometer was shaken, scrutinized and popped under Sue's tongue. Her arm was bandaged and squeezed, the cold of a stethoscope in the angle of her elbow.

'OK, Mrs Bennett.' The smile was wide, friendly, the almond eyes impish. 'Those bits of you are normal, so you're cleared for today's visitors.'

'Can I have a mirror?'

The nurse hesitated, then smiled. 'I'll check with Sister, but it should be OK. After all, it's less sedation from now on. Time to get back in the land of the living.'

It was a shock for Sue to see the travesty of a face reflected back at her.

'Coming on nicely,' Sister informed her firmly. 'The swelling's subsiding and the bruising developing well. There's been a big improvement in the last twenty-four hours.'

The nurse tidied the bedclothes and smiled, her eyes sympathetic. 'The bruises will soon go yellow and be less obvious,' she assured Sue. 'Until then, how about some make-up?'

Her parents had come and gone frequently and this morning they were her first callers. There were fresh nighties for Sue, and cologne for her hair which her mother brushed gently and with love. Pippa and Ken were questing faces at the door and the Lavins welcomed them before leaving Sue's room in search of coffee.

Pippa had an armful of jonquils, Sue's favourite flowers. There were tears threatening to rise as she remembered Colin buying all he could as long as the season for them lasted.

'Is there anywhere left to put them?' Pippa asked with her throaty laugh, while Ken began to move vases round, trying to create space.

'Someone's spent a bob or two on this little lot,' he said as a formal arrangement of late spring flowers defied his attempts to make them share their table top.

'I can guess,' Pippa grinned at Sue.

It had been from Sam, together with such a stiffly written note Sue wondered if he had found it difficult to do.

'These are sweet.' Pippa bent her head to the fragrance of primroses. 'They could have come from children.'

Celia had sent them after Adam and his sisters had denuded the garden. 'They did,' Sue croaked. She was surprised to hear her own voice again.

'The flat's OK,' Pippa said. 'We had the odd newshound at the door, but your editor sent Kate Jeffries to deal with them. She came to us afterwards, demolished half the gin and seemed to think you'd make a good article.'

They did not stay long, their ration of Sue's time enough to tire her. The ward sister arrived to check on her patient and listed the phone messages. 'Mostly from a Mr Haddleston, and Mr Beamish,' she said with a twinkle.

Sue did not rest for long before the door opened and Paula appeared with a posy of freesias, their daintiness as appealing as their scent. Her schooling had taught Paula the social niceties and she regaled Sue with snippets of information from the *Journal* offices until they were interrupted by an aide with a tray of hot, beige soup.

'Get well soon,' Paula said quietly, gripping Sue's fingers before she left.

'Who was that, darling?' Mrs Lavin asked. She had returned with her husband, passing Paula in the corridor.

'A friend from the *Journal*.' Sue surprised herself, realizing it was true.

Mrs Lavin helped her daughter sit up, shaking and pushing pillows until she was comfortable and could reach the trolley across her bed. Sue spooned the soup. The warm, thick liquid did nothing for her taste buds, but it eased her throat and she realized swallowing was becoming marginally less painful. Her parents sat beside her bed and were pleased to see faint signs of returning colour in her cheeks.

Sue was anxious for them, they looked so tired and drawn. 'Now I'm on the mend, you're to go home,' she said as firmly as she could. 'You've got to get some proper sleep.'

When they protested Sue reached for her pad and pencil, scribbling orders that they were to stay home for two days. 'Have enough nighties to last that long', she wrote. Her mother read the words, then went reluctantly home to Dorking.

A porter did his round with newspapers and Sue beckoned to him for the *Journal*. Reading it was like being back home. Kate was as scathing as ever about a pseudo-blonde willing to tell all for a fat fee from another paper. Cary was busy hinting at two possible divorces which would leave horse-mad elderly men the poorer. Paula had turned in a good column on hay-fever research.

It was Jonah's article which haunted Sue long after she stopped reading. He echoed Watty's style, describing the terror endured by survivors of a massacre. The murderer had been released, choosing to go back and live where he had caused such devastation. For the families of his victims the horror had returned. Once more they were exposed to the full force of evil.

Sue let the paper fall from her fingers. How would she feel if James Rocket was free and living in the next street? The idea appalled and she knew blind panic until the quiet of the room, guarded by a policeman, convinced her she could go on breathing, even dare to move a little.

She looked out of the window, watching blue sky being chased by cheeky clouds. It looked so peaceful up there. With droves of staff between her and the outside world, Sue was safe. No unwanted visitor could reach her.

The day progressed with its regime of checks and notes, drinks and ignored food. With fewer drugs Sue still dozed, but more lightly. Sounds were louder, smells stronger, and she reacted quickly each time the door swung wide, sinking back against her pillows when the incoming nurse or doctor smiled.

As Sue drifted in and out of sleep time trickled away. Lunchtime was a battle with stew and rice pudding, but she was defeated and they congealed accusingly, earning Sue tuts and disapproval.

In the early evening a huge armful of irises hid Kate. She demanded vases from the nurses as her eyes raked Sue, checking that all was well.

'Five minutes they've allowed me! I ask you. Five minutes for me to talk?'

There was gossip from the office, of Jepson home at last, a posse of nurses to care for him.

'And every one horse-faced,' Kate said with glee. 'You've got to hand it to his wife, she knows the old bastard. It looks as though Sam might keep his job,' she went on. 'Circulation's up since he took over, so the money men are behind him. In this day and age that's what counts.'

Sue heard of Cary, his wife threatening to use a sharp knife to good effect if he did not forswear blondes. Sandy had yet more photos of the twins, their christening the affair of the decade. Jonah, coughing badly, was carrying on Watty's fight to get justice for victims.

As Kate's voice drifted away Sue realized her concentration span was not what it had been. Kate saw the hollowing of her friend's cheeks, the pallor. She leaned over, kissed Sue gently, then went away without another word.

Lights were switched on and the room was a bright

cell giving it a sense of isolation which Sue welcomed. Strangers passed, visitors on their way to help patients fill an hour before the last hot drink and a sleeping tablet.

The door opened and she looked up, hearing a nurse warn against tiring Mrs Bennett. Sam strode in, armed with a stack of magazines. Above them his expression was one of deep concern. Behind him walked Miles, red roses in abundance. Sue recalled the parody of a face she had viewed in the mirror and began to chuckle. Two gentlemen callers, as her granny would have said, visiting a girl whose face was a swollen mask above bright purple bruising.

Sam followed Sue's glance behind him and glared at the intruder. Miles stood his ground, merely raising a quizzical eyebrow at the anger he was engendering. Sue watched the two men and a long-ago memory returned. She was a student at Slimbridge, quiet in a hide there and watching two males in a flock bristle and strut in competition for a dowdy hen duck.

The animosity between the two men was tangible. Sue gave them her best smile and settled back to enjoy the encounter. The past receded, the present was increasingly free of pain and drugs. As to the future, it suddenly seemed to promise fun.

'Have you two been introduced?' she asked huskily.

Names were exchanged, hands shaken.

Sam, thrusting as ever, took the lead, laying the pile of expensive print on the high trolley that served as Sue's table. 'In case you get bored,' he told her. His eyes raked her face, trying to reassure himself she was recovering. 'Celia sends her love, so does Peter. She wanted to come today but it's a long way for her from Blackheath and Adam's not well.'

'Serious?'

'No. Chickenpox.'

'Girls next.' Sue had learned to ration her words.

'They've had it,' Sam said, a little more cheerfully now

he was holding a private conversation in a room he felt was over-peopled.

'Give them a big hug from me, and thank them again for the flowers.'

Sam moved a chair close to Sue's bed, determined to stay as long as possible. Miles took the opportunity to put the roses down on the bedside cabinet. 'I wanted to make sure you were OK,' he told her. Grey eyes watched Sam sit four-square, his arms folded belligerently, then he smiled at Sue. 'I'll get in touch when things have quietened down. Meanwhile,' he said, his eyes merry, 'no talking to strangers.'

Once Miles had gone, leaving the room oddly empty, Sue lay back against her pillows. She listened to Sam as he talked of the *Journal*, the latest stories that could not be printed, of D notices and writs, irate politicians threatening to sue for libel. It was easy to let the pleasant voice wash over her while she hooked snippets that intrigued from the flow.

Sam was sensitive to Sue's exhaustion and left early, but not before bending to kiss her. His eyes searched hers as he stood again, looking for hope. She did not know if it was there for him, but he smiled, content.

Sue closed her eyes, shutting out the world and the fear it held for her. There was the creak of a handle. She looked up and saw Gerry. 'I'm so glad you've come.'

'I had to see for myself. Richard said you'd be finding hospital food hard to swallow, so I brought a little concoction.'

From the bag he was carrying came a dainty bowl, a spoon, a linen napkin. A wide-necked thermos was lifted out and opened. The aroma of the broth which was poured from it made Sue feel hungry and she sat up, expectant. It was as good as it smelled, the fusion of ingredients heartening. Sue realized Gerry must have spent much time and thought to get the balance of texture and flavour right. He earned his appreciation watching Sue scrape the last

193

drops from the bowl before she relaxed with a sigh of satisfaction.

'How did you know that was exactly what I needed?'

Gerry became a little pink, so he took off his spectacles and polished them, hiding his eyes. When the shining lenses were back protecting his thoughts, he looked at Sue. 'I just put myself in your place, wondering how you'd feel. Richard told me what your muscles could and could not do, and what your digestive system would be crying out for. I'm just glad it worked.'

Sue put out her hand to him and he held it, the undemanding warmth of contact breaking down the barriers of her fears. Tears welled up, Sue making no attempt to hide them or brush them away.

Gerry did not move, waiting for her to take the next step. At last Sue sniffed, raising her free hand to wipe away the moisture. Gerry used a tissue from the box beside her bed, carefully drying cheeks and eyes as he would have tidied a child. That done, he smiled at her.

'Oh Gerry, I'm so sorry.'

'Why? It was what you needed. I just feel very privileged to have been here with you.'

'You understand so much. I don't have to explain things to you.'

'Explanations aren't necessary – but you need to expose what it is you fear. Only then can it be dealt with.'

Sue flung an arm over her head, hiding her face with her arm in a curiously defenceless gesture. Gerry waited, patiently still in his attempt to be of help.

'You've made such good progress,' he said at last. 'The doctors say you'll be home soon.'

'I can't.'

The words were muffled, but Gerry heard the misery in her voice. 'If you can't face going back to the flat, why not stay with your parents? You'd be thoroughly spoiled there.'

The head under the sheltering arm was shaken, an element of violence in the action causing Gerry to frown, be concerned.

'What is it, Sue?' he asked, the gentle tones easing under her guard.

'I'm so scared.'

'That's perfectly reasonable. I would be more worried about you if you weren't frightened,' he assured her. 'What scares you? Exactly.'

The quiet in the room was accentuated by the sound of a trolley being pushed along the corridor outside. Two of the porters were talking, their words indistinct, their laughter fading.

'Happening again,' Sue said so softly Gerry had to bend his head to catch the words.

'You mean the possibility of this character reaching you a second time?'

Sue nodded.

'That I can understand, but let's examine the facts. Rocket's locked away, he can't get at you. There are charges against him which are going to stick, however good a defence lawyer he hires. For once there is good forensic evidence. If nothing else does it, his DNA will convict him.'

The body in the bed was immobile, listening.

'Are you afraid of seeing him when the case gets to court?' Gerry probed.

Nothing, then Sue took in a deep breath which ended in a sob.

'I think anyone who has endured what you did must have reservations,' Gerry went on, his tone even, 'but you must decide. Rocket committed a crime against you. Does he go to prison for it, or do you?'

'Me?'

'Yes, you. What else do you call shutting yourself away behind locked doors? It's where he deserves to be, not you.'

What Gerry said made sense, so much sense, but Sue was tired. Had she strength enough to fight?

'Then, of course, there's Colin,' Gerry added. 'If you believe this Rocket killed Colin, shouldn't you do something about it?'

The hand above Sue's head came down and plucked at the sheet. 'Gerry, it's awful,' Sue confessed. 'I keep thinking of Colin, remembering so many things about him.'

'But?'

'I can't see his face.' Sue expected Gerry to be shocked, but his smile held serenity.

'It happens. It was the same with me after Damon was killed. I went walking in Cumberland, thinking I'd tire myself out and sleep, but it was no good. I was so wrapped up in myself I couldn't even see Damon. In the end I went back to work and in the evenings looked at all the snapshots we'd taken, remembering the good times. Those memories never disappear.' He paused, his thoughts deep, private. 'Have you a photo of Colin here?'

She shook her head. Gerry gently released his hand and pulled out his wallet. Sue sat up, pushing hair back from her face, then reached for a tissue and blew her nose resolutely.

Gerry held out a snapshot to her. 'Remember? That time Richard wanted to try out his new camera?'

The four of them had had a pleasant evening. The food had been miraculous, then Sue and Colin had been seated on the sofa while Gerry knelt behind them, Richard rushing into place at the last moment before the flash went off.

'Can I keep it?'

'Of course,' Gerry assured her. With deft movements he packed away the picnic remains.

Sue stroked Colin's face. He was back with her.

'I must go.' Gerry was apologetic. 'Richard's been working too hard. He was called to theatre in the night, then it's been clinics all day. I've left him a meal, but he won't eat it until I'm home.'

'When you met Richard, and wanted to be with him,' she said slowly, 'did you feel disloyal to Damon?'

196

There was a brief sadness in Gerry. 'At first. Then I realized what I felt for Richard had a life of its own, and it took none of my memories of Damon. When all's said and done, what else is there when someone's gone?'

With no drugs to numb Sue dreaded being part of the bustling existence of real life. When she left the hospital on legs suddenly shaky, she was driven the short distance to her parents' home and her old room. Everything was as it had always been, yet each picture seemed to be of a man with deep set eyes under a hat of some kind. Whenever she moved Sue could sense hot breath on the back of her neck while she waited for the clutch of fingers around her throat.

Mrs Lavin was disturbed because her daughter refused to see any callers. Sue found it better to hide away in her room and stand with her back to the door until she heard farewells and the clang of the garden gate. Attempts to persuade Sue to help her father in the garden fell on deaf ears. For her fresh air did not mean waxy cheeks regaining health, it was the medium in which terror grew until it eclipsed the sun.

For two days Sue's anguish climbed until she could bear it no longer. She had to escape from the house in Dorking. Her parents drove her to Islington, staying with her while a locksmith was called. Workmen came and went, Sue fretting over each tiny delay until new bolts were fitted. The windows were made impregnable and small surveillance cameras installed to show anyone appearing at the front door, or climbing the stairs.

Safely locked inside her fortress Sue's tension lessened, but her parents' constant concern irritated. It was noticed by Pippa who persuaded them to leave, promising to be on call. Unhappy, Mr and Mrs Lavin went home.

Alone at last Sue prowled the flat, constantly checking no one was hiding there and that each lock was firmly in place.

Pippa was worried. She knew her friend's state of mind was due to exhaustion as much as experience, but there seemed to be no way Sue could get the long, deep sleep she so desperately needed. Suggestions of doctors, counsellors, drugs even, were all vehemently rejected. Only the locks were important.

'This obsession with security, Sue. For heaven's sake, the man's in jail.'

'And if he escapes? There's no hard evidence to tie him into Colin's murder, only my word. He'll come for me.' Sue paced the room like the caged animal she was. 'If he doesn't, someone will – and it's only attempted murder for me, remember. If Rocket just stands trial for that, even if he's convicted, he'll be out in no time.'

'Why not go back to your parents? You could get some peace and quiet there.'

'No!' Sue turned, pleading with Pippa and wincing as she did so. She rubbed the side of her neck, still feeling the pressure of fingers. Polo-necked sweaters could hide the bruising, but muscles and soft tissues sent their own messages, reminding her of damage and the stream near the railway line. 'No,' she said more quietly. 'That's where he got me last time.'

'Then let me stay with you, at least until the trial.' Pippa smiled, the effort a little lop-sided. 'If you must keep yourself imprisoned, at least it needn't be in solitary confinement.'

'What about Ken?'

'Ken will understand. He'll help.'

'Help baby-sit me, you mean.' Sue tasted again the bitterness of being helpless.

Sam bombarded Sue with phone calls and persuaded her to start work again.

'You can do it from home,' he reasoned, 'and it'll save the hassle of coming in until you're ready'

It was a comfort to sit at the terminal in the safety of her home and gradually join in the life of the *Journal*, even at a distance. Anil was back in the office and helping Paula.

'Getting on like a house on fire,' Kate gossiped on one of her frequent phone calls to Sue.

There were many messages from Miles in her e-mail. Each one was brief, light-hearted, and Sue found herself smiling as she read them, wondering how he managed to find time to do any work.

Sam called at the flat with a fresh stack of magazines and a hopeful expression. He wanted to take her out for a meal, break her away from the confines she imposed. Sue refused, preferring to share with him dishes from the freezer.

'It's getting to you, isn't it?' Sam said gently, unhappy with her gaunt frame and haunted eyes.

They were stacking plates in the dishwasher and Sue inched away from Sam's nearness. Since the attack, with the exception of her father and Gerry, she could not bear to be touched by a man, any man. The male workers in the hospital had seen her withdrawal from them. Used to the reaction they had merely called for a woman doctor or nurse. Sam, too, understood, but he lacked their patience.

'Why not go and stay with Celia?'

'No!'

The unexpected violence of the answer shocked Sam. 'Why not?'

'The children would be in danger,' Sue told him, a little lamely.

'It's more than just that, isn't it?'

Sue buried her face in her hands and Sam reached out comforting arms, but she pulled away from him, running to her bedroom and sobbing behind the slammed door. Defeated, Sam called his 'Goodbye' and left.

Sue sealed the flat behind him and surrendered to her fears, crying with the wail of a lost child. When the sound ceased she was exhausted, kneeling by the couch and clutching a cushion for comfort. Sue patted it smooth and replaced it, ashamed of what she had become. After Colin's death it had been just possible to get through each

199

day with a little dignity, but now the panic attacks which hit her with repeated suddenness had taken away her spirit.

'Adrenaline, it's only excess adrenaline,' her scientist's mind argued, but the rest of her had been turned by Rocket into a helpless mess.

'Talk to someone,' the clinical voice inside her head urged silently, but she was afraid to tell anyone of the abject terror waiting for her once she left the safety of the flat.

A thousand times a day Sue told herself it was just her imagination which peopled the street outside with Rocket, or others who were Chester's men, but her mind would not listen. It was too scared to hear.

Miles progressed to phone calls, keeping his tone light, the conversation undemanding. Unlike Sam he did not try to intrude, but he did attempt to persuade her to talk to a psychologist friend. He had no more success than anyone else.

Kate was more blunt when she brought gossip and champagne. 'Sue, if you don't get some sleep soon, real sleep, you'll crack.'

'I'm all right. There's nothing wrong with me.'

Kate marched her to the bedroom and made Sue look at herself in the mirror. 'Say that again.'

Sue picked up a brush and dealt with her hair firmly. Kate was right, but it was impossible to tell her about the dreams destroying her sanity whenever she let sleep take hold.

'I'm fine,' she insisted. 'Just fine.'

Stephen brought Louise and Sue warmed to her immediately. Louise was not unlike her, Sue thought. They were the same height, both slim and dark, with similar regular features. Their hair marked the difference. Sue's swung free, while Louise had her dark brown hair smoothly coiled in a French knot which gave her an air of serenity.

'I wanted to meet you,' Louise told Sue, 'but Stephen wouldn't let me – until today.'

'The time we talked on the phone,' Sue's mind was back in the past, 'you didn't want me to come back to the flat. Why?'

Louise looked down at her hands, the knuckles white. She moved her fingers, easing them before she looked at Sue. 'I had a sudden feeling of darkness.' There was no need for more.

'And when I said I was going to Dorking?'

'There was light, and yet I could hear water rushing over my head. In the distance a dog was barking.'

There was a quiet stillness in the room. Sue watched Stephen put his hand over Louise's and squeeze gently.

'And now? What do you see now?' Sue had to know.

Louise met Sue's look squarely, her green eyes candid. 'Now, I don't sense danger near you but,' she hesitated, 'it's in you.'

'What do you mean?' Sue insisted while Stephen frowned, uncomfortable.

'I don't know,' Louise said simply. 'Perhaps you do?'

Sue thought for a moment, facing a harsh fact. 'It's my own fears that are harming me?'

'Something like that.'

Strangely reassured by Louise, Sue was a little more at ease, but the locks and cameras remained fully used. Sleep was still snatched periods of letting go before nightmares reared, leaving her to wake with a start. Each morning Sue would be numb for seconds, waiting for muscles deep in her viscera to contract. Her heart then began its pounding and pulses raced while she shook and sweated, sick with mindless terror.

Movement helped, but ordinary chores were not enough to occupy her mind and body. Sue persuaded Pippa, with

Ken's help, to carry in pots of paint. Redecorating the bedroom gave her body a legacy of aching, but eventually curtains hung spring-fresh at windows which gleamed with new paint, clean panes.

Television played an increased role in her life. The science programmes she had always watched, but now Sue left the set on most of the day. The voices and activities provided company, interest, from people she could dismiss with a single switch. They did not threaten the fragile peace in her mind.

When Sue was restless she had to use muscles bathed and overdosed with the adrenaline of fear. Sam kept her busy, memos coming thick and fast to the flat and demands for copy increasing. Not all was printed and Sue guessed he was doing his best to work her to recovery. It was not enough.

In the middle of a furious polishing of the dining table a news broadcast caught Sue's attention, a hospital mentioned. Sue had heard whispers on the grapevine of gossiping scientists and realized the hospital had at last gone public with its research findings. Using computers in the laboratories, their medical team had been able to track and use individual healthy sperm in men of low fertility. 'Poor Jepson,' she chuckled out loud, 'too late.' Probably just as well for Mrs Jepson, she thought as she turned back to her polishing. If the bimbo had produced a son, Mrs Jepson would have been cut away willy-nilly.

'An investigation has begun into the death in custody of a remand prisoner,' the well-modulated voice of the news reader informed her. 'During a scuffle which broke out as prisoners were being returned to their cells, the man fell and received head injuries from which he has since died.'

There was a pause, then, 'In Birmingham, the latest of the statues to be erected in the city centre –' Sue switched off the set.

She was stunned, unable to think clearly. Hope began to surface and she pushed it away. It was immoral to want someone dead. Even a man who deserved to die, a small voice whispered in her mind?

'Don't be so stupid,' she told the image reflected back at her from the shining table. 'Of all the men on remand, why should it be him?'

Did she want it to be Rocket lying dead? It was a question she wearily shied away from answering. A longing to be safe, at peace, rose until Sue ached with it. She reached for a photo of Colin, seeking reassurance from the smile fixed in time. They had argued and reasoned until their beliefs were sound, founded on logic as well as humanity.

Calmly deciding someone should die was murder, they had agreed. Yet it happened daily, Sue admitted to herself. Terrorists made it part of their creed and a mistake merely earned an off-hand apology the community was supposed to accept. Doctors were faced with constant dilemmas. With too few organs for transplant, too few resources, too many patients, which should survive?

Survival. The word rang round Sue's tired mind. Colin had been the strong one, she the weak, but it was Colin who had died at Rocket's hands. She paced the flat, willing the phone to ring and bring information. Silence.

Unable to wait, Sue found and dialled the number of Martin Lawrence's chambers, demanding to speak to him. He was in conference, a thin, nasal voice informed her, but a note would be made of her request and she would be contacted when Mr Lawrence was free. Sue tried to talk to Stephen. 'Out', she was told curtly before she resumed her pacing.

The phone rang and she darted to it.

'Rocket?' Martin Lawrence said after he had listened to Sue's impassioned outburst. 'Rocket. Not a name I've encountered, I'm afraid. On remand, you say?'

'Yes.' Sue was almost shouting in her anxiety.

'Then there's no way he would have come up for consideration by us, even if our little organization had still been functioning.'

'You've stopped?'

'Since Watson Skinner's death. Yes.'

Sue put down the phone and tried teletext. All that was reported she already knew. Jonah was appealed to, but he had no extra information.

Ready to scream she heard Mrs Willoughby's voice. 'Work through it,' echoed in her head. Sue collected a bowl of hot water, added detergent and scrubbed carpets. She was exhausted by the time the kitchen floor, too, had been scoured and polished and Stephen rang her door bell.

'It was him?' she demanded to know as she held open the door.

Stephen walked in and closed the door behind him. He took Sue's arm, leading her to the couch, making her sit.

'It was Rocket?'

Stephen stood for a moment, then sat beside her. 'Yes, it was.'

She closed her eyes. Relief washed through her, cleansing, healing. 'An accident?'

'Oh, I'm sure the police report will read "accidental death". I gather he started the fight, though what provoked him no one's saying. A lot of punches were thrown, one way and another, and he went down, banging his head. Or it was banged for him.'

'You think –'

'One of the officers who broke up the fight and tried to get help for Rocket heard the word "weasel".'

'The same kind of execution he used to carry out himself,' she shivered. 'Live by the sword and you die by it?'

Stephen lifted his shoulders expressively. 'It was his world.'

'But who set it up?'

'My guess is Chester. I've been talking to a friend who was one of the team interviewing Rocket. They wanted all they could get on Chester, so they pushed hard.' He smiled, a grim effort. 'As hard as the rules allow. There was enough evidence to convict Rocket as the man who had attacked you, but he was the only one who could have linked in Chester. Remember, it wasn't only your husband's death Chester ordered, and probably Skinner's as well, he was behind a whole host of crimes, none of them minor. My guess is Chester was tipped off the net was closing. He scarpered just in time.'

'Peter Tym's picture,' Sue reminded Stephen.

'That was a lucky shot, and proof Chester hoofed it in comfort. Still, it must have upset Jimmy Rocket. I gather he was furious with his friend Paul for clearing off to Spain and leaving him behind. Rocket had a blind loyalty to Chester, and needed someone to blame for the desertion. That was when he focused on you.'

'Something I could have managed without,' Sue said bitterly.

'Chester had been sharp enough to realize you had access to Colin's notes and he was the one wanting you scared off. Unfortunately friend Rocket wasn't very bright, and probably decided it was your fault Chester ran, not because the serious crime squaddies had him in their sights. In what passed for Rocket's mind, you had to pay,' Stephen told Sue, keeping his voice gentle. 'He had difficulty getting to you when you were on your own. When he did, he got caught.'

Sue put her fingers to her throat. The pain had gone, but its echo remained.

Stephen knew he must lay all the ghosts haunting Sue. 'There was always the danger for Chester that once Rocket was banged up he might be angry enough to sing like the proverbial canary. Even if he thought he was safely out of England, Chester couldn't take the risk. He needed Rocket dead.'

There was a strange ringing in Sue's ears, a blurring of images. She shook her head, trying to clear the miasma. She wanted to crawl away, disintegrate. Instead, she forced herself to be calm.

'Can't Chester be stopped?' Sue hoped she did not sound as wobbly as she felt.

'Yes, but police methods take time. Let's face it, he'll use the law to protect himself.'

'Watty used to say it's the criminals who get the justice.' She smiled, remembering kindness. 'I tried to get him to stand for Parliament and get a victims' justice bill passed.'

'It's about time the balance was redressed,' Stephen agreed. 'Meanwhile, the old type of retribution has to do.'

'What do you mean?'

'I've heard a whisper there's a contract out on Chester. Someone's keen to take over his little empire – and his profits.'

Sue heard again the roar of a white car, saw spurting gravel and the flash of leopard skin. 'His wife? She's a tough one.'

'And then some.' Stephen's grin was wry. 'She's been seen with an upwardly mobile young tearaway. They're both greedy and she's ruthless enough for two. I wouldn't mind betting she'll use him to keep Chester's interests intact when she's a widow, and the boss.' He sighed. 'Our job will be to watch it happen with our hands tied behind our backs, then clean up the mess.'

Weariness threatened to engulf Sue. She knew now who had killed Colin and why. His murderer had ceased to exist and her fear of giving evidence had been so much wasted energy. There would be no trial to face, no chance of Rocket tracking her down. Not ever.

Difficult tears slid down her cheeks. As they increased, the tightness which had been inside her since Colin's death began to unravel. It was like a dam being breached. First the oozing, then small jets, finally the cascade as the barriers fell away.

Stephen was patient, letting Sue cry, holding her when the sobs shook her body. The storm began to pass. Calmly practical, he gave her his handkerchief.

'Will you be all right?'

Sue could barely see him through her swollen lids, but she sensed his concern. 'I'm just so tired.'

Her exhaustion was total. She lay back on the couch, limp, unresisting, her fears gone.

Stephen swung her feet up and around, helping her to lie more comfortably. 'Shall I get Pippa?'

Sue shook her head and, reluctantly, Stephen left her, but not before fetching a blanket and covering her as she lay on the couch.

It was so quiet, Sue thought, so peaceful as night darkened the room. She just wanted to sleep. In the shadows she sensed Mrs Cahill and Mrs McGovern, Mrs Porter too. The silent watchers nodded to each other.

At last, she understood.